THE LAST HOMELAND

MATTEO RIGHETTO (b. 1972) lives and works in Padua, at the b___ r of the _____ ___ any of his works tak___ __ce in beautiful mountain lan___ ___es that he knows deeply, having visited them since childhood, backpacking with his father. *The Last Homeland* is the second book in the trilogy which began with *Soul of the Border*, also published by Pushkin Press.

THE

LAST

HOMELAND

MATTEO RIGHETTO
TRANSLATED FROM THE ITALIAN BY HOWARD CURTIS

PUSHKIN PRESS

Pushkin Press
71–75 Shelton Street
London WC2H 9JQ

First published by Pushkin Press in 2020

Published by agreement with Piergiorgio Nicolazzini Literary Agency (PNLA)

1 3 5 7 9 8 6 4 2

ISBN 13: 978-1-78227-481-0

Designed and typeset by Tetragon, London
Printed and bound by CPI Group (UK) Ltd, Croydon, CR0 4YY

www.pushkinpress.com

To those whose homeland is the wind, the forests,
the clouds and the water in the rivers.
To those whose homeland is the dawn,
the sunset and the starry sky.
To those whose homeland is justice and loyalty.

The moon was rushing through the clouds; now nothing seemed to exist any more but laments.

MARIO RIGONI STERN,
The Sergeant in the Snow

Then it come to me clean as spring rain. Life is just what it is, and it ain't fair at all.

JOE R. LANSDALE, *The Thicket*

PART ONE

1

S TEALTHILY, THE TWO MEN lay down on the ground, chilled to the bone but silent as lurking snakes, careful not to be seen or heard. They lay still for a few minutes, while the tops of the spruces around them slowly swayed.

From the edge of the woods, surrounded by bushes of withered raspberries and big scattered leaves of meadow dock, they watched him as, without a care in the world, he explained to his son how to shoe a horse.

Augusto De Boer, little Sergio and Samson were twenty or thirty metres further down, windward of them. The two men watched Augusto, then turned to each other like two excited predators and exchanged conspiratorial sniggers.

At this point Augusto's wife came out, soon followed by his elder daughter.

The two men lying there did not bat an eyelid.

Walking as quickly as ever, Agnese went over to the woodpile and picked up some ten or so beech logs, then said something to her husband and son, who both answered her.

The two men in the woods did not catch this dialogue, even though the wind was blowing in their direction.

Jole bent and picked an autumn crocus, put it over her left ear and went up to her father and little brother. She stroked Samson and kissed him on the brow. She said something and the three of them smiled, although immediately after that she said something to her father that seemed like a reprimand.

She was more beautiful than ever, her long flowing hair as bright as hay gathered from the meadows, her skin burnished by the late summer sun. Just from the look in her eyes, it would seem that the future was on her side and had made an everlasting pact with her, like the pact between time and the beauty of the surrounding woods and mountains, both rugged and sublime.

The thinner of the two men, half his face deformed by a severe burn, slowly took off his felt hat and whispered:

"Four."

"Huh?"

"There are four of them left. The other daughter hasn't been there for a while."

"One less," murmured the other, fatter man, who had a scar on his right cheek, bloodshot eyes and eyebrows like a wild bramble bush that could have served as a vipers' nest.

"Yes. Now we need to find out where he hides the stuff. We'll have to be patient."

They smiled and waited quite calmly for all the De Boers to go back inside the house. Only then did they slowly get up and return to the woods behind them. After about a hundred metres they came to a small secluded clearing amid a dense, tangled thicket of downy oaks and a few felled and already decaying conifers. Using big knives, they cut some hornbeam boughs and, weaving them with chestnut branches, erected a refuge that looked like nothing so much as a fox's lair.

They went inside it and sat down, bathed in sweat. The thin man took a bottle of grappa from his knapsack, knocked back a swig and passed it to the other man.

"We have to be patient," he repeated.

The fat man drank and said nothing. The patch of early November sky visible above them was clear. The air was cold, dry and thin, imbued with the scent of resin.

The thin man searched again in his bag and finally took out some pieces of aged and smoked rabbit meat. He ate one and gave another to his accomplice.

A strange noise suddenly rose above the rustle of the woods. Repeated calls, a series of harsh, muted clicks.

Teck... teck... teck... tock...

The two men stopped chewing and looked around.

Teeek... tock... tock...

A shadow flew low over them. The grouse hovered for a moment then disappeared beyond the felled trees, perhaps in search of its mate.

Suddenly, after a few seconds, there was a strong and unexpected gust of wind from the north that rustled the leaves of the trees. The wind blew the felt hat off the thin man's head and sent it rolling along the ground.

The other man laughed. Then the wind died down. The thin man recovered his hat and the two men resumed eating.

2

T WO SUMMERS HAD PASSED since Jole had crossed the border, found her missing father and returned home with him.

Two years may be a long or a short time, depending on a host of things, starting with the place where we live.

By the autumn of 1898, the De Boers were the only family still left in Nevada, that tiny village in the grim mountains between the Asiago Plateau and the Brenta Valley, the only family to have determinedly resisted the idea of leaving their own land and emigrating because of hunger.

For some years now, a genuine exodus had been under way. From the Dolomites and from every corner of the Venetian Prealps, the peasants were abandoning their houses and pouring down into the valley like streams in the May thaw. Masses of the poor, forsaking their country in search of a better place.

In ten years more than a hundred thousand people had left the Veneto. There was almost nobody left up in the mountains. That spring alone, three hundred and forty-three people had departed from the Brenta Valley, all of them ending up on the other side of the world. The emigration agents promised good times and full bellies, emphasizing that those who arrived at their destinations first would get better accommodation.

And this had happened in Nevada, too. In the last ten months, first the Zests and then the Battistas had gone, leaving the De Boer family alone and more isolated than ever.

Augusto, despite the temptations held out to him by the "promisers" – the name given in these parts to the emigration agents who climbed all the way up here promising new paradises – had chosen to stay where he was born and had grown up, convinced that better times for everyone would come sooner or later. On the few occasions on which he talked about it, his arguments were weak and half-hearted. Every now and again, Agnese would wonder if her husband was really convinced of what he said, seeing that things were going from bad to worse. Even Jole disagreed with him, but was forced to accept his stubborn will.

The life of the De Boers had continued, but with struggles and sacrifices that were sometimes unbearable, especially since Augusto had decided to stop smuggling his tobacco over the border. For quite some time now he had been selling only small quantities down in the valley, as almost everyone had done until just a few months earlier. He had decided to put an end to the difficult, dangerous journeys, which may have allowed him to glean some precious metals, but only by risking his own life and that of his eldest child.

The days and the seasons succeeded one another, never changing, measured out mostly in the laborious rituals and rhythms of tobacco cultivation and the traditional simple life of the poor. And as if the injustices perpetrated by the Tobacco Company were not enough, taking away the crop every year and paying almost nothing for it, in mid-August two terrible storms had destroyed a large part of the planted area, battering it with violent winds and hailstones as big as chestnuts. Larvae and parasites had done the rest, nibbling away at the last surviving tobacco leaves. At about the same time, Judith, their one remaining cow, had died of tetanus, as had Mos's black horse, which Jole had brought home from the journey across the border, but which she had never wanted to give a name. The horse's muscles had started to contract and within a few hours the increasingly frequent spasms had risen all the way to its neck. It had found chewing difficult and its nostrils had become increasingly dilated. Less than a week after the appearance of the first symptoms, it had bowed its head and died. The same fate had befallen Judith only two days later.

Fortunately, at the first signs of that fatal illness, Augusto had made the decision to isolate both animals in order to prevent Samson's becoming infected.

Once they were safely dead, he had dug a big hole a few hundred metres from the house, thrown the bodies in and burnt them.

Sergio had been very fond of Judith: it was he who fed her and generally took care of her under his father's watchful gaze. When he had seen her in the hole he had been unable to hold back his tears.

Jole had drawn him to her and hugged him, all the while watching the black horse burn inexorably in the flames, the last witness to a time and an adventure that had largely remained a deep, unfathomable secret. She had watched it burn with eyes full of compassion, but without feeling any nostalgia, as we watch an ugly memory fade away for ever, carrying with it the stench of our most unpleasant experiences.

Augusto had filled the hole and within a short time buttercups and clovers had grown over that patch of ground, yellow and green as the colours of the most beautiful of seasons.

3

DESPITE HIS STRENGTH and his proverbial solidity, even Augusto, surrounded by all these terrible difficulties and burdened with responsibility for his family, had begun to show the first signs of decline. Since returning home with his daughter he had aged rapidly. He was only forty-six, and yet the thick moustache he wore proudly had turned almost completely white. His back had become slightly stooped, and the skin on his face and arms, although as hard as the bark of a larch, had grown dry and furrowed.

Over the last fourteen months, he had been forced to draw on the little treasure he had amassed from his former illicit trade with Austria-Hungary. In order to survive with dignity and to support his nearest and dearest, he would go down to Bassano to barter a few ingots of silver and copper in exchange for provisions.

And so it was that, by early November 1898, only the last eight ingots, four of silver and four of copper, remained in his secret hiding places beneath the meadows near the house. Although Augusto had always hoped that one day they might serve as Jole's dowry, deep down he knew that soon, perhaps as early as the following spring, he would have to dispose of them, too.

Jole had turned twenty a few months earlier. She was a woman now, and was growing ever more beautiful in spite of her isolation from the world and the sacrifices and difficulties that life up there imposed on her.

She was as tall and strong as a birch, and like a birch she rose in search of as much light as possible, constantly trying to silence the past and find a little peace. It wasn't easy, and lately she had become increasingly nervous, apathetic and unmanageable. She worked hard on the *masiere* and in the vegetable garden with her father and mother, but as soon as she could she would get away and walk barefoot in the woods or roam with Samson in the pastures of Rendale, blending into the nature around her, feeling part of it. Riding through forests and across meadows calmed her, gave her a sense of joy that she had not felt within the walls of her house for some time. She needed to be alone, and often found fault with what her mother and father said. She clashed with both, but especially with Augusto. Was there really no other way to get by? she would argue. There must be something they could think of that would allow them to live with more dignity. Whenever they argued, Sergio said that they were like two stags locking horns. Sometimes, when her father refused to listen to her any more, Jole would escape to a meadow, lie down on the grass and look up at the clouds racing across the sky above her, changing form and aspect. She would remember the past and wonder if everything she had lived through had really happened. But when images of her adventure came back into her mind her doubts vanished, and a kind of anger would begin to throb in her soul, a wild force ready to burst out, like a rocky crag that breaks loose from a mountain face and crashes down to the valley in all its destructive power.

Galloping on Samson or walking barefoot on the soft moss or in the icy water of a stream, she felt happy. Yet she would have been ready to do anything, even use force, to fight the abuses and injustices that oppressed the weak. Not so much because her father had taught her this,as because she had been taught by life itself, and her adventure two years earlier. An adventure that had stamped itself into the furthest recesses of her consciousness.

4

JOLE'S YOUNG SISTER, Antonia, who loved to create pen-
dants by embedding insects and flowers in resin, had left
them more than a year earlier, in the spring of 1897.

Increasingly influenced by and imbued with her mother's
religious faith, she had undergone a spiritual conversion as
strong as it was remarkable, and had soon decided to devote
herself to God. Everything had begun gradually, when she
had started spending ever more time in her room, kneeling
beneath the image of the Virgin. Then, as the weeks passed, her
devotion had manifested itself more intensely, until it occupied
most hours of the day. Antonia had stopped spending her free
time in the woods or playing with her little brother and had
dedicated herself entirely to prayer and contemplation. She
had started going on frequent pilgrimage to the little church
of San Francesco in Foza. Augusto had been a little upset
at first, but in the hope that his daughter's spiritual inclina-
tions might somehow reach the ears of God, he had silently
accepted the change.

Agnese was as happy as a mother can be to see one of
her own wishes coming true in her child. As far as she was
concerned, what was happening to Antonia was the will of
God, and she saw her sincere conversion as a kind of bless-
ing. Jole, too, had seen a true light in her sister's eyes and had

been quite shocked by it in a way, because she herself did not feel that light inside her at all and was even somewhat alarmed by Antonia's behaviour. Sergio, for his part, was losing a playmate and a friend, someone with whom to enjoy carefree diversions on the rare occasions when they managed to put aside their work.

The day Antonia told her father and mother that she had decided to enter a convent and asked them to go with her to Bassano was one of the most important and moving moments in the life of the De Boers.

It happened one evening in late spring. The hours of daylight had already increased considerably and the sun's orange and gold rays entering through the kitchen windows remained until the dinner hour, when the family gathered around the old walnut table. They had just finished saying grace over a bowl of cabbage soup.

"Amen," they concluded in unison.

After a few moments' silence, Antonia, her head bowed, said in a timid voice:

"Papà, Mamma – I want to become a nun."

Augusto fell silent and continued eating, as if he had heard nothing.

Agnese, holding her breath, turned abruptly to her husband, then looked at Antonia and again at Augusto.

Jole heaved a deep sigh, entranced by the golden rays of the sunset.

Sergio ran his hands through his hair and asked in astonishment, "So you want to go away?"

In truth, they had all been expecting it. Each of them

knew that sooner or later this moment, these words would come, but they had not known when. Now the moment had come.

For a minute or two nobody said a word. Agnese was the first to speak.

"Are you sure?" she asked in an anxious voice.

"Yes, Mamma."

Augusto finished eating his soup before looking at her. "My girl—" he began, but was interrupted.

"Papà!" Antonia cried.

"Don't say a word," he said, his voice firm but calm. "If you're really sure, we'll go down to Bassano tomorrow and see if we can talk to someone."

Antonia made the sign of the cross, leapt from her chair and ran to hug her father.

"God bless you, my daughter," Agnese said with tears in her eyes.

Hard as it was for her to understand her sister's choice, Jole appreciated the great sincerity, the ardour with which she had come to that decision. She herself envied her certainty, her unshakeable conviction. It was only now that she realized how much Antonia had changed, what a different person she was from the playmate she had been. But it was also yet more proof that her father, who had become increasingly severe and irritable towards Jole, was always lenient and understanding towards her sister and her brother. And she did not understand why. Why did he never listen to her? And yet now, in the twilight of the day, behind the hard and apparently impenetrable shell of his character, he had shown himself capable of understanding her sister's heart. Jole had learnt in her life that really being able to listen to someone else is one of the most precious talents that can be found in a person.

And Augusto had that talent. But not with her.

5

"HE'S ONLY AFRAID of losing you, my daughter, don't you see that?" her mother said to her one evening while the others were all outside, smoothing her long blonde hair by candlelight with a comb made from a roebuck bone. Jole had asked her mother if she could talk to her.

"Afraid of losing me?"

"Oh, my dear, you've grown. You don't know what it means to be the father of a girl like you."

"Well, you don't know what it means to be the father of a girl like me either."

They laughed. Agnese gently turned her daughter's head and looked her in the eyes, stroking her hair and gazing at her with all the gentleness of which a mother is capable. It was as if they were in another world at this moment, in a dimension without time, without pains, without problems, and there were no such things as hunger, hard toil, backs broken by work in the fields, humiliation from the Tobacco Company's collectors, uncertainty about the future. None of that. Only the two of them, love, tenderness and hope conveyed through the eyes. And the more they looked at each other, the more they recognized themselves in each other's faces, as in a kind of journey through time. In this almost magical moment, past and future disappeared, merged in an eternal, happy present concealed in Jole's constellation of freckles and in her mother's fingers as they moved delicately to outline her face.

"One day you, too, will learn what it means to be with a man," Agnese said.

"Yes, but who knows when?"

"It'll come, Jole, the time will come," Agnese said, once again combing her daughter's long hair, which was just the way hers had been when she was young. "And don't provoke your father," she went on. "You're the child he's most attached to. It happens, you know."

Jole closed her eyes and snorted.

"The thing is, he's as stubborn as a mule," her mother said by way of conclusion, lightly kissing her on the head.

6

J OLE HAD KNOWN LOVE the previous year, although obviously she had not told anyone.

The experience had overwhelmed and confused her sensitive yet vibrant, combative, fiery, lynx-like spirit.

His name was Sebastiano, and she had seen him for the first time while roaming the woods in spring. He was a tall young man with black hair and large eyes. She had ridden past him on Samson, passing within ten metres of him, and he had turned to look at her, removed his cap and given her a big smile. Jole had turned red, but the next day she had gone back the same way at the same time just so she could enjoy another smile like that, all for her. And that was what had happened. On the third day he had greeted her in a beautiful, confident voice, and she had dismounted.

"My name's Sebastiano. What's yours?" he had said.

"Jole."

He was the same age as her, belonged to a family of Cimbrian origin and came from Rotzo. He worked as a seasonal *pechér* for a landowner in Asiago. His task was to bark a few thousand black pines to extract coarse resin. He would cut a V on the best trunks and with great care, patience and skill gather the *péch* oozing out, the resin from which his employer would make turpentine and rosin to sell to merchants down in the plains.

Since that day, the two young people had encountered one another several times in the woods, but Jole had never again had the courage to stop and talk to him. Once, though, she had brought him some blueberries she had gathered during the ride and in return he had given her some *péch* to chew: he had put a little resin on a warm metal plate and tilted it so that the resin ran down slowly and became purified as it did so. The result was a kind of scented rubber, which was nice to chew. That was the day he embraced and kissed her beneath a larch.

For days, Jole had felt confused and unsettled, yet happy. Then, two weeks after that first kiss, he had told her he would be leaving, as so many of his contemporaries were doing.

"I'm going to America," he had said in a low voice, his eyes fixed on the ground. "My whole family are moving there."

After these words he had tried to embrace her but she had broken away and looked at him, her eyes watery with disappointment and resentment.

She had been unable to say anything, even though she would have liked to scream in his face how much she despised him for having treated her like this, as if she were nobody, without even asking her opinion of his plan to leave for America.

She had got back on Samson and galloped home, cursing the resin, the *péch*, and all the *pechérs* in the world, who mortally wounded trees to exploit their precious scented tears.

7

ONE MORNING AT DAWN, with Jole, Sergio and Agnese starting work in the *masiere*, Augusto had tied Samson to the cart and gone down to Bassano with Antonia to visit the city's convents.

In the evening, soon after sunset, they had returned home tired but satisfied. They had visited all six convents in Bassano and Antonia had immediately opted for the Augustinian nuns in the old convent of San Girolamo, where she would enter as a postulant and then become a novice.

The following week, after more days of prayer and reflection, they had made ready to go down again to Bassano, this time to fulfil her vocation and have her accepted once and for all by the community of nuns. Agnese had gone with them, so happy and so moved that by the time Augusto had yanked on Samson's reins to get moving, her eyes were brimming with tears. Antonia would not be so far away, and she would be making a dream come true, her dream. Jole and Sergio, though, had no desire to be separated from her and see her go. They had said goodbye outside the house. Because when it came down to it, this really was goodbye.

8

I T WAS EARLY AFTERNOON on a day in mid-November 1898.
Jole had only just come back up from the River Brenta,
where she had helped her mother to wash clothes, while Sergio
and his father had been on the tobacco terraces since dawn,
trying to complete the work before the winter break. At this
period, it was necessary to get rid of the stalks of those plants
that had remained in the *masiere* after that year's wretched and
disastrous harvest. The work required a lot of time, because it
was necessary to gather the stalks one by one, cut them and pile
them in big bundles or sheaves, to be burnt the following year.

High, thin clouds drifted across the sky, white but tinged
with all the colours of the rainbow, depending on how the sun
was reflected in them. Jole left the house and walked past the
shed, on the roof of which grew a wild blackthorn, full now of
blackbirds, fieldfares and song thrushes. She crossed the vegetable
garden and headed for the spruce wood to the south, the only
patch of green in the autumnal palette of broad-leaved and
deciduous trees. A few paces from the first trunks, she stopped
to breathe in the solid scent of wood, fungi and moss issuing
from the forest like the exhalation of some ancestral spirit.

She plunged into the forest with the respect every worship-
per observes entering her own church, and a few paces further
on sat down on the huge tangled roots of an imposing spruce.

She stopped to listen to the calls of a great tit, a wheatear, a skylark and a yellowhammer.

She smiled, got up again and walked further into the forest.

She had always loved being here, walking the paths, venturing into hidden corners, thinking, reflecting; but ever since she had made that epic journey two years earlier, it really was as if breathing in these smells and this silence had become a kind of necessity, a daily ritual without which she could not be at rest.

She thought about her sister. Since she had shut herself up in the convent, Jole had been able to see her only twice, for a few hours. The first time had been at Easter, when the mother superior had allowed Antonia to spend a few hours with her family, and the second time on the Day of the Dead.

After a while, Jole gave a kind of start, and a strange vibration went through her body, from the tips of her toes to the top of her head. She came to an abrupt halt and looked around. Her survival instinct, akin to that of a wild animal, put her on her guard. It was as if there were something mysterious around her. But even concentrating all her senses, she did not see or feel anything strange.

A few dozen metres away, motionless and well hidden behind the felled trunks and the leaves of meadow dock, the two men watched her, careful not to move a single leaf, almost holding their breaths.

Jole stood there on the alert for a long time, like a wary doe, sure that her presentiment had not led her astray.

Then she picked up a pine cone half-peeled by a *schirata*, the red squirrel common in that place, and slowly retraced her steps.

"Pretty girl," murmured the man with the burn and the felt hat.

"Huh?"

"Fine figure of a woman!"

"Oh, sure, fine figure of a woman!" the fat one exclaimed with a smile. "But I reckon she's more poisonous than a viper."

"Well, I eat vipers raw!" The first man laughed triumphantly.

When she left the wood, Jole looked again at the sky, which was slightly duller now. The sun was dimming and in a short time its rays had become softer and more oblique.

Hundreds of starlings spun about in mid-air, performing acrobatics and abrupt pirouettes, describing incredible figures that Jole amused herself interpreting, just as she had interpreted the clouds in summer when she was a little girl.

9

THAT EVENING, putting the polenta on the table, Jole asked if they too had seen the starlings in the sky.

"They were making incredible patterns!" she exclaimed. "I've never seen so many before!"

Agnese and Sergio had not noticed them, but Augusto had. Nothing ever escaped him.

He sighed, his thick white moustache moving as he bit into speck rinds with some dried-out *puccia* bread. "I saw them," he said wryly. "And I also cursed them."

Jole looked at him incredulously, waiting for him to explain his words.

"It's like when there are too many wasps in summer. It's not good," he went on, still chewing and looking down at the plate in front of him. "It's not good," he repeated.

"Why?" asked Sergio, who had a lively, curious nature, as if some sprite had given his body all the energy in the world.

"The old folks used to say they bring long cold winters. Not much snow and a lot of ice… if not some harsher curse!"

Agnese made the sign of the cross and looked anxiously at her husband: she knew that the old peasant proverbs were seldom wrong, just as she knew that a winter with not much snow but a lot of ice was a lot worse than an illness.

Sergio, though, as light-hearted as ever, huddled even further down on his chair and, taking care not to be seen by his mother, touched himself three times, amused by his own gesture.

Jole did not open her mouth. She could not bear the fact that her Papà could not – or worse still, would not – see the world with any kind of imagination. She would have liked to answer him in kind, saying that the flight of those birds was a wonder and that at least they could do what they wanted. But she bit her tongue for fear of how he would react.

They all fell silent. The only sound was that of their slow, patient chewing.

"May God bless us," Agnese sighed after a train of negative thoughts.

"That's the only thing you ever say!" Augusto retorted. "Maybe he should bless us a bit more, don't you think?"

"What do *you* think?" Agnese replied resentfully.

Sergio laughed, but his mother glared at him.

Jole closed her eyes: she had no desire to see the usual scene.

For a moment she thought about how long this life would last, these days that were all identical, this self-denial, these sacrifices, this hunger, this constant struggle with the cold. She dreamt of leaving, finding a boy ready to marry her, making a life for herself, a home. And yet something kept her here, in this house with the *meléster*, the mountain ash, amid her family. A kind of curse. It was as if she, too, had put down roots like a tree and it was impossible for her to uproot herself and set off into the world in search of something that was hers alone.

But I'll be leaving soon, she thought.

All of a sudden, Sergio said:

34

"I'm going up to Campomulo tomorrow for the mountain pine."

It was rare now to find mountain pine, with its low, creeping branches, because what the shepherds had not yet eradicated in order to extend the areas of pastureland had been gathered by the mountain peasants to sell to the kilns in Nove and Marostica in return for a little money or, more frequently, a little flour. And one of them was young Sergio.

He went there often to gather mountain pine. Walking tirelessly, clambering beyond every pasture and every stone quarry with the agility of a chamois, he had discovered a completely unexplored little area where the trees grew in profusion and spread their branches over the whole ridge. It was his secret place, and he had learnt to love it as much as the little hill near the house from which you could see the winding stretch of the River Brenta and listen to its roar as it drifted down into the plain. He would go to Campomulo at least once a week, stay there from dawn to dusk, and come down with two huge hemp sheets on his back filled with that scented plant.

"Good for you, son!" Augusto would say on his return, and slap him on the back.

Apart from helping his father in the *masiere* and gathering mountain pine, Sergio did thousands of other things, among them collecting the dark tannin that formed in oak apples, or else stockpiling cones from the tallest conifers, especially in years of abundance, when nature seemed to burst with fruit.

Collecting the tannin was easy and not at all risky: all you had to do was cut off the oak apple, extract the dark liquid and pour it into a mess tin. Augusto would then sell it down in the valley, to be used as ink. As for the pine cones, they were required of the De Boers by an important carpenter in the area, and would eventually turn up in the houses of well-heeled families of the Venetian and Paduan bourgeoisie as Christmas decorations.

Compared with collecting tannin, gathering pine cones was particularly difficult and dangerous: to procure a reasonable number, you had to climb to the tops of the conifers and jump like a *schirata* from one tree to the next, and you risked falling more than twenty metres.

Sergio did so with total unconcern, like all the young mountain boys of his age, because not only was he a clever child, he was also cocky. They all were at the time. And if you weren't that way already, you soon had to become so.

10

A T DAWN THE FOLLOWING DAY, while Sergio was on his way to Campomulo, Augusto checked up on the places where he kept the ingots hidden. He did so periodically, as if to reassure himself that all was not lost, that there was still some hope of getting by while waiting for better times.

Just then, the man with the burn woke his companion, who was asleep in the undergrowth, wrapped in a hemp blanket.

"I think we've identified all the places now," he said with a smug smile. "The rumour about him was definitely true."

The other man roused himself abruptly: even though he had caught only the last words, he had grasped the meaning of the whole sentence. "Great!" he said, rubbing his rough, stubby hands.

"Let's go down to my mother's and rest up for a few days. We'll definitely be back next week."

11

S ERGIO RETURNED HOME later than usual. It was dark and Agnese had been so worried that she was waiting for him in the doorway of the house. She could not take her eyes off the grassy hill her son would have to descend. When by the light of the almost full moon she saw a small figure in the distance approaching the house, she ran to him, fearing that something was wrong. And in fact her sixth sense was right. When she reached him, she embraced him and asked in a tense voice:

"Where have you been all this time?"

But Sergio did not reply. Instead, he dropped the two sacks full of mountain pine and fell heavily onto his mother in a faint.

"Augusto! Jole!" she called in the direction of the house, highly agitated. "Come quickly! He's not well!"

While Jole gathered all the mountain pine that had spilt from the sacks, Augusto loaded Sergio on his back and carried him into the house. Agnese immediately stuffed the stove with beech logs and put a nettle infusion on to boil.

Sergio still wasn't speaking. They laid him down on his bed and by the light of two candles noticed that his eyelids, neck, wrists and ankles were very swollen. They undressed him and examined his whole body. He had no wounds or signs of wild animal bites. It was impossible to tell what had happened to him. All three tried to keep calm and let him rest, hoping it was only a reaction to excessive physical effort. They stayed with him, Agnese and Jole sitting on the bed and Augusto remaining on his feet, to one side. Feeling Sergio's brow and seeing that he had a high fever, his mother started praying.

And they all prayed until the following morning, but the situation did not improve. Even though he lifted his eyelids slightly, Sergio showed no sign of recovery.

Agnese and Jole laid cold compresses on his forehead and gave him various infusions to drink, but despite this care there was no improvement. On the contrary, the fever kept rising.

"What do we do?" Jole asked her mother.

"He has to rest and keep drinking infusions of arnica and nettles. Apart from that, we have to pray to the Virgin."

"We can't just pray, Mamma!" Jole said.

Just then, Augusto came into the room. He gave Sergio a good look, examining his neck and hands again, and seemed reassured.

"Let's not worry too much," he told them. "It's almost certainly a spider bite." He lifted Sergio's hand and showed them a little ulcer on the tip of his right index finger. "It'll pass."

"And what if it doesn't?" Jole asked in exasperation.

Her father looked her straight in the eyes. "I said it'll pass."

Agnese stepped in to calm them down. "Let's wait until tomorrow morning. If he's not any better then, we'll take him down to see the Holy Woman in Oliero."

"No!" Augusto said bluntly.

Agnese sighed. "Apparently the woman knows how to solve problems like these. She's a healer, or something like that. A good Christian, anyway, so they say."

"She won't be any use," Augusto said. "Sergio will pull through anyway."

Irritated by her father's stubbornness and worried about her brother, Jole had no intention of giving in. "I'll take him!" she cried.

"You'll not take him anywhere!" Augusto retorted angrily.

"Calm down, both of you," Agnese said, raising her voice.

"Mamma, there's nobody left in Nevada now," Jole said, "but do you remember what the Battistas told us about this Holy Woman? How she cured one of their sons of an insect bite? Do you remember? Why don't we take Sergio to her?"

"We don't even know where to find her," Agnese said.

"We just have to go down to Oliero and ask!" Jole said. "Even the stones in the river must know where to find the woman!"

"We can talk about it again tomorrow, daughter. In the meantime let's hope he gets better without needing to take him all that way."

"He's not going anywhere," Augusto said, cutting them short. "If he was bitten by a hook-legged spider, which is what I think, it'll take a few days, but then he'll be as good as new. Sergio is going to pull through!"

12

D URING THE DAY his condition did not improve, nor
did it do so as night approached. All at once Sergio also
started to have convulsions and his body, already boiling hot,
became covered in sweat and red spots. Towards midnight the
repeated cry of an eagle owl set off a loud echo, and Jole felt
a shudder run down her spine.

As the hours passed, there was no lessening of the fever and
the swelling of the body did not go down. The owl continued
to hoot for hours on end, flying about near the house until
the first light of day, when Augusto put two logs in the kitchen
stove, donned his worn old jacket and his hat and went out
beneath a fine drizzle to gather the *rega*, the weeds, that needed
burning and to spade the virgin soil on the tobacco terraces.

Agnese and Jole had taken turns resting so that at least
one of the two should always be at Sergio's bedside. Agnese
mostly prayed, while Jole constantly replaced his sweat-soaked
compresses, wetting his lips and spreading his chest, wrists and
ankles with her mother's arnica ointment.

"We have to take him down there, Mamma!" Jole asserted.
After some time, she was exhausted and losing patience.

"Didn't you hear what your father said?"

Jole clenched her fists and her mouth. "Sergio's sick! What
if it isn't a spider bite like he says?"

Agnese sat down, hunched over. "Do you think I'm not worried, Jole? But we have to keep calm. I trust him. Your father has never been wrong."

"I'll go!" Jole cried.

"Where?"

"To see this Holy Woman. I'll go, and I'll go now!"

"That's enough, Jole!" Agnese said, but without conviction.

At these words Sergio moved his eyelids and for a few seconds opened his eyes slightly. His gaze seemed murky and distant. Then he turned to the other side and dozed off again, and his body stopped shaking.

"Can't you see he's already better?" Agnese said. "Why are you so stubborn?"

"I'm not stubborn, I'm afraid my brother could die! You're the stubborn one, Mamma, though not as stubborn as Papà!" She burst into tears and rushed out of the room, where the stale air already stank of fever and illness.

Agnese looked at the old walnut crucifix on the wall. The suffering face of Christ seemed alive and real. Her eyes came to rest on the crown of thorns pressing down on his head and brow, causing drops of blood to ooze out. She murmured something, her lips moving imperceptibly, then looked at her son lying on the bed, bathed in sweat, and finally at the crucifix again.

"Have pity on us," she whispered, and closed her eyes.

In the meantime, Jole had already taken her Haflinger horse from the shed and quickly tied him to the cart. In a short space of time she went in and out of the house several times, carrying woollen blankets, hemp cloths and water.

The early morning sky was low and compact, its clear grey colour lending it a sad uniformity. It felt a little warmer compared with the previous days, but a fine drizzle was falling in tiny, bothersome droplets.

She came back inside out of breath and ran to Sergio's room. Heedless of her mother's astonished reaction, she went to her brother, took him in her arms and carried him outside. She laid him gently on a layer of blankets and covered him in such a way that he would be still and well protected from the air and the bad weather.

"What are you doing? Are you mad?" Agnese cried, running after her, but not really trying to stop her.

"If you don't want to take him to the Holy Woman, then I will!"

In a furious hurry, she put on her old leather boots and her thick white jumper of Feltrino wool, tied her red kerchief around her neck and pulled her usual big straw hat down on her head.

"I'll be back!" she cried.

She got on the cart, resolutely seized the reins and, without further ado, cried "Ya!", urging Samson to get going.

Her mother put her own body in the way to stop her. The expression on her face, though, became all at once imploring and pitiful, as if in the end she would surrender to her daughter's will.

"Give me a moment at least!" she said categorically, raising one hand, palm outward. She lifted her long skirt with both hands and ran to the hen coop behind the house. A few moments later, she returned, holding a red hen by the legs. "You don't want to go empty-handed, do you?"

Jole smiled.

In no time at all Agnese tied the hen's legs with a short length of twine and placed it in the bed of the cart.

"Now you can go. And may God bless Sergio, and you, too, you obstinate girl!"

Her daughter blew her a kiss.

"Yaaa!"

The horse reacted immediately to Jole's command, and the cart wheels groaned as they pulled free of the mud that the rain and damp had already made of the ground.

Agnese watched her as if approving of and envying her daughter's courage, though she would never have admitted it.

"Your father will be angry! Oh, yes, very angry!" she whispered, making the sign of the cross as Jole rode out of the yard.

Jole turned and looked her straight in the eyes. They were watery, filled with her great humanity.

Samson advanced slowly at first, then broke into a trot. Within a short time, the cart was already at the edge of the ridge, and beyond it began the winding forest road leading down to the Brenta Valley.

From the other side of the hill, Augusto had witnessed the whole scene, but had not moved. He stuck the pitchfork in the ground and leant his chin on the handle, waiting to see how it would all end up.

Then he took a plug of tobacco from his trouser pocket, stuck it in his mouth and started to chew it calmly, his moustache moving like the top of a larch battered by the wind.

"I'll deal with you when you get back," he muttered as he watched the cart go over the hill.

44

He seized hold of the pitchfork and plunged it straight into the sheaf of *rega*, thinking as he did so that this year his tobacco plants had brought him nothing but sorrow and frustration.

"That girl is as stubborn as they come," he said, landing another blow with the pitchfork. "That's also why I love her... And it's why she'll go far."

13

BARELY TWO MONTHS EARLIER, Jole had asked her
father's permission to go alone to Asiago for the festival
of San Matteo, a traditional celebration that for centuries had been held on 21 September, on the occasion of
the annual transhumance of the flocks from the summer
pastures.

To this joyful festival, which attracted a large number of
people, the shepherds brought and sold not only goats and
sheep, but also everything they had produced during the
months of pasture: cheese, wool, tools, materials.

Jole loved the festival and had been several times, sometimes
with her father, sometimes with the whole family. They had
never had enough money to make large purchases, but they
had always managed to barter, like so many peasants from the
surrounding mountains.

That year Jole would have liked to go alone, and stay all
day, to enjoy a change of scenery and join in the traditional
games held on the Asiago Plateau, attracting a lot of young
people like her.

There were days when being in the house with the *meléster*
weighed heavily on her and at such times, which were increasingly frequent, she felt the need to see different faces, meet
new people, speak with someone her age. In short, to have a

little fun, like all the young men and women of the plateau and the Brenta Valley.

On the morning of 19 September, two days before the festival, Augusto had been bent over the dried tobacco, tying it into identical bundles, while Jole had just finished gathering potatoes and was standing there in front of him.

She told him her intention of going to the festival, convinced that her father would not find fault with it.

But Augusto remained silent.

She repeated her request.

He stopped, looked up at her and said no, she couldn't go.

This time she fell silent. She could not believe it. She asked him why.

He replied that he did not have to explain or justify himself. She couldn't go, and that was it.

Jole clenched her fists. For a moment, she really felt as if she hated him. She ran out of the barn and burst into tears. In her anger she kicked a bucket filled with potatoes, knocking it over and spilling all of them.

Agnese, who was piling firewood, heard the metallic noise of the bucket and saw her daughter looking desperate. She called to her and reprimanded her, but Jole took no notice, continuing to climb the hill with nervous, rapid steps, mentally cursing her father and his eternal pig-headedness.

Agnese went into the barn and joined her husband.

She asked him what had happened.

He ignored her, sticking a plug of tobacco between his teeth and continuing to tie the matured leaves with twine, handling them with care in order not to damage them.

She asked him again.

Augusto said that Jole would not be going to the fair.

Agnese looked at him with an imperturbable, resigned look, observing him as she would have observed the rocky face of a mountain that has not changed in centuries.

She tried to make him see reason. "She's grown now, and soon she'll have her own life. You can't pretend she won't."

But he did not react.

She left the barn, lifted the hem of her long skirt and quickly climbed the little hill.

She found her daughter sitting on the ground, crying. She was torn. On the one hand she could no longer bear certain aspects of her father's behaviour; on the other she felt shame and a deep sense of guilt: he was her father, and she could not think badly of him.

Agnese stroked her head and ran her hand through her long hair, as blonde as wheat.

Jole jerked her head back, refusing the contact. She got to her feet and moved a few metres away.

Agnese said nothing, but calmly, patiently, approached her again.

She stroked her hair once more, and at this point Jole raised her head. She looked at her mother's compassionate eyes, and swiftly but humbly flung her arms about her neck, hugged her tight and wept even more, letting go as she would not have done with anyone else these days.

14

JOLE URGED HER HORSE on so that he should advance swiftly but without jolting the cart too much.

It was almost eight hundred metres from the house with the *meléster* to Oliero, all downhill.

The route that led from Nevada down to the valley was not impassable, like the old smugglers' tracks, where a cart could not go a single metre without overturning or getting snagged on the branches of the trees. But it was still a narrow, badly maintained road, made up mostly of laid stone and packed earth, which became very slippery whenever it rained. Jole alternated between keeping her eyes on Samson and turning to look at her brother. Despite the unavoidable movements of the cart, he was quite still, well wrapped in the blankets and sheltered by a curtain Jole had placed there to protect him.

The sky grew darker and the descending clouds enveloped and swallowed parts of the deciduous forest, muting the bright colours of the last leaves still clinging to the branches.

The rain grew heavier and, despite the broad-brimmed hat shielding her face, Jole often had to wipe her eyes and cheeks with the back of her hand to rid them of the drops of water that prevented her from seeing where she was going.

She kept thinking of how much her brother must be suffering, and she knew she would have to get to her destination as quickly as possible and find the Holy Woman, her one hope of curing the boy.

Bend after bend, jolt after jolt, she soon began to hear the noise of the river beneath her, that River Brenta so beloved of Sergio and so important in the history and the daily lives of the people of these lands. Guiding Samson and watching over the little body behind her, Jole thought again about the decision she had made, the gravity of her action.

For the first time in her life she had dared to disobey her father, and what was more, in such a difficult situation.

She had never before had the courage to cross the border between her own autonomy and her father's authority.

Augusto had known it would happen sooner or later, it was in the nature of things, in every generation, and so it was with Jole. She too, had known it would have to happen sooner or later, that sooner or later she would have to act on her own initiative, even if it meant going against her parents' wishes. Now, descending from Nevada in the rain, it hurt her to think about this. But she felt she had done the right thing. She had had no choice. Urging Samson on, she repeated to herself mentally that she could not have waited even another hour to see if her brother might get better. She had not wanted to run the risk of seeing him die without even trying to help him.

Rivulets of water and mud had formed and ran down along the edges of the road. The puddles were getting bigger with every passing minute, as though trying to conquer all the available space. Out of the corner of her eye, Jole spotted a roebuck just inside the woods to her right. Despite the rain, it stood impassively beneath an alder, nibbling at fern and liverwort. Jole envied its calm and serenity. She turned to check on Sergio.

All around there was a strong smell of mud and sodden earth, mixed with the typical smell of rotten, decaying leaves so common on rainy autumn days. More bends, more twists and turns, a few slight slippages, and at last the descent came to an end.

Less than an hour later, she was down in the valley. Soon afterwards, she was in Valstagna, and then on the outskirts of the hamlet of Oliero.

15

"HOW BEAUTIFUL YOU ARE, my daughter!" her mother had said to her, plaiting her long blonde hair.

"I don't really think so, Mamma…"

It was an evening in early summer, a few months earlier. Jole and her mother were tired, having worked all day. Augusto and Sergio were still out on the *masiere*, but would be back shortly. Mother and daughter had already lit the stove, chopped the vegetables and put the copper saucepan on the fire to make the minestrone they would be eating for the next few days. Particularly since Antonia had entered the convent, the two of them had often got together and shared a few moments of closeness, woman to woman.

Whereas Sergio, who was everybody's pet, was ever more drawn to the figure of his father and tried whenever he could to spend time with him, his sister, as she grew, felt the instinctive need to rediscover her mother's humanity, to consult her, to have a sense that she was with her at this delicate time in her life. And whenever she felt this way, as if by some unwritten law of nature, they would seek each other out, without necessarily using words. They grew ever closer and gradually began to discuss the same matters, without raising any barriers but, rather, reaching a perfect understanding. After a few gestures or a look, their sympathetic collaboration would end with a sentence or a word that would open the way to a moment of closeness, of female intimacy. And the secret moment between mother and daughter always culminated in an affectionate gesture. Agnese might comb her daughter's hair or rub cream of martagon lily and saxifrage on her hands, which were cracked and lined from her work in the fields. Sometimes, though, it was Jole who took care of her.

And they talked together, exchanging compassion and comfort rather than ideas about life.

"No, you are beautiful!" Agnese had exclaimed, stopping her plaiting and tilting her head back to look her in the face. "Never doubt it, Jole. Do you understand?"

Jole had smiled at her gently.

"Of course," Agnese had added, "it isn't beauty that matters in life, but it can help sometimes, you know."

"What about you, Mamma? What did you think when you were my age? What was your dream?"

Agnese went back to plaiting Jole's hair, lovingly, patiently, while she thought of the right answer to give her. "What did I dream?"

"Yes. What did you hope for from life?"

Raising her eyes to the window that looked out on the woods, Agnese had sighed. "I dreamt that I wouldn't have to suffer the way I saw my mother suffer. I wanted a better life than hers..."

"And did it work out that way, Mamma?"

Agnese had pretended to think this over and then lied. "Of course. My life has been better than my parents'."

Jole had not believed her but pretended she had, because she knew that lie made her mother feel better.

Agnese had resumed plaiting Jole's hair.

"And do you think mine will be even better than yours, Mamma?"

"That's for sure, my daughter. Oh, yes, for sure!"

Jole had smiled in satisfaction. "I don't know. I think about it a lot but I don't know. You're only saying that because you love me."

Just then, the front door had been flung open and Augusto and Sergio had come back in.

The two women had cut short their conversation and resumed making dinner.

16

T HE FIRST THING SHE DID was command the horse
to stop. Then she climbed into the cart to see how her
brother was.

Jole was soaking wet, but luckily Sergio was dry, the curtain
having protected him well from the wind and rain. She moved
the hem of a blanket which had moved up over Sergio's face
during the ride and was relieved to see that her brother was
fast asleep. The convulsions had gone. She stroked him and
touched his forehead. The fever had not gone down.

"Be patient a while longer, little brother," she whispered
to him.

Within minutes the rain thinned out, then stopped altogether.

It was early morning and, apart from the constant roar of
the Brenta as it carried all the rain and residue of the last few
hours from the Sugana Valley and the border, there was no
sound, not even the repeated, metallic noises of blacksmiths
at work.

Jole got back on the cart and urged Samson on towards the
main part of the hamlet. After another two hundred metres,
she entered the main square and turned into an alleyway.
Outside the church of Santo Spirito she saw a large gathering of people, both men and women. She leapt down off the
cart and ran towards them. When she reached them she saw

that there were even more of them than she had thought at first. They were thin, sad and unkempt, exhausted from hours of waiting. Many were silent, others were praying out loud, others still were intoning nursery rhymes and lullabies. All were tense and worried.

"Good morning!" Jole said to a woman. She was dressed in black, with a dark shawl around her head that left only a small part of her grey, lined face visible.

"Good morning to you," the woman replied, seeming confused. She looked deep into Jole's curious eyes. "We're going to America," she said in a dejected tone.

Whenever Jole went down into the valley and realized how many people were leaving these mountains, this land, she felt a sense of profound loss.

She took a deep breath, turned for a moment to look at the cart where Sergio was lying and then, trying to dismiss these thoughts, asked the woman if she knew the area.

"Yes, I'm from Valstagna."

"Do you know someone they all call the Holy Woman?"

She nodded beneath her shawl.

"My brother is sick and I need to find her right away!"

The dark figure raised an arm, reached out her hand and with a thin, bony finger pointed to a dilapidated old house with peeling walls, wedged between the Brenta and the face of the massif opposite, beyond the bank.

"That small grey house?" Jole asked.

"That's the one!"

Jole gave a little bow of gratitude. "Safe journey... and good luck!" she said, turning to retrace her steps.

"Thank you, my girl. May the Virgin bless you and your brother."

Jole ran to the cart, gave Sergio another glance and commanded her faithful Haflinger to set off again, straight to the house of the Holy Woman.

17

W HEN SHE CAME TO THE SMALL, run-down building the migrant had indicated, Jole got down off the cart, grabbed the red hen by the legs – the bird was moving about, squawking and flapping its wings – and looked around for the front door.

She summoned up her courage and knocked vigorously.

After a few seconds the solid wooden door creaked open and Jole found herself face to face with a middle-aged woman with short hair, wearing grey clothes and a long apron woven with floral patterns. Someone in another room was playing a mouth organ.

"What do you want?" she asked without wasting any time.

Somewhat intimated, Jole said, "I'm looking for the—"

"The Holy Woman!"

"Is that you?"

She laughed. "Me? No, girl, I'm just here to open the door and greet people." Then she leant slightly beyond the door and peered into the street. "That horse and cart yours?"

Jole nodded.

"Put them in the back yard, then come inside."

"But my brother's in the cart, he's the reason I'm here!"

"Can he walk?"

"No, he has a high fever."

The woman snorted. "Then it's best he's helped by the Holy Woman's son. At least that way he can do something useful." She turned towards the interior of the house and called:

"Ruggero!"

From inside came a harsh, resentful voice in response.

"There's someone out here who needs loading on your back!" she yelled.

The same sharp voice now cried:

"Strim, come with me!"

The music stopped.

The woman stepped aside. Behind her two men could be seen coming to the door.

As soon as the light hit their faces, Jole felt disgust and embarrassment at the sight of them. Ruggero was a thin man, with half his face peeled and twisted by a burn that had deformed part of one ear and his mouth. He was wearing a thick leather jacket, a felt hat and around his neck a big grey kerchief, which he kept adjusting in a kind of tic.

Strim was big and fat, with a deep scar on his cheek and eyebrows joined in a single strip of thick black hair. His typical shepherd's clothing was filthy and he stank like an Alsatian dog after two months in the rain.

When Ruggero put his face outside the door and saw Jole he gave a start, but pretended nothing was amiss and turned to his companion.

"What is it?" he asked the woman.

"In the cart. There's a fellow who needs taking out."

"He's my brother," Jole said.

"Leave it to us." The Holy Woman's son looked at her calmly, sure of himself. Strim was about to play his mouth organ again, but his companion stopped him.

"That's enough of that! Don't you ever know when to stop playing?"

Strim put the instrument in his pocket and loaded Sergio on his back, his strange boots leaving big pointed prints in the mud of the yard.

Sergio had opened his eyes and seemed to be wondering what was going on. Jole, still at his side, tried to reassure him with her smile.

A gust of wind blew her hat to the ground. Jole bent down to pick it up and noticed the two men's filthy, mud-stained boots, especially the pointed prints left by the fat one's soles.

Ruggero and Strim carried Sergio inside and carefully laid him on a straw pallet.

"Now you can give me that hen," the woman said, holding out her hand. "See that door over there? That's where the Holy Woman is. When she calls you, just go in – though, as you can see, there are a few people before you."

She seized the hen from Jole and went into the Holy Woman's room.

The two men went out, saying nothing, closed the front door behind them and quickly headed for the stable behind the house.

"Now's the time!" the first man said.

"Who'd have expected that, eh?" the other man replied, laughing coarsely.

They hurriedly saddled their horses, and before long galloped off beneath a sombre, murky sky.

18

"HOW ARE YOU FEELING?"

Jole stroked Sergio's head, and he looked at her dreamily. He was finding it hard to keep his eyes open.

She took the canteen tied to her belt, opened it and poured a little water on his lips. She took a sip, too, looking around her.

The room that seemed to serve as a waiting room was narrow, with damp, flaking walls covered in dark green mildew. Along one wall, five people were sitting on chairs stuffed with straw, waiting to go in. There were four other chairs, all empty. The five who were waiting their turn, four women and one man, seemed absorbed in their own worlds. This one stifling his pain, this other one weeping, a third huddled in desperate prayer.

God alone knows how many people have been through here, Jole thought, looking at the empty chairs as if ghosts were sitting on them.

She raised Sergio from the straw pallet, holding him in her arms. He was burning hot.

"You'll be better in a while, Sergio. Just stay strong!"

She looked at the door behind which was the woman who had caused her to disobey her father.

He'll understand… she told herself. *He's bound to understand…*

A thousand thoughts and fears were going round and round in her head, but above them all were a sense of urgency and the uncontrollable yearning for that door to open.

She had to keep waiting, though. She stroked Sergio and, in her way, prayed to God to remember her family.

Why do we poor wretches always suffer? Why? she kept asking herself. *And why we do always have to endure the abuse of those who take advantage of our poverty? Where is your justice, God?*

After almost three hours of waiting she was now alone. At last, after a few more minutes, it was her turn. The door opened and Jole was able to see the Holy Woman.

She had expected to meet a kind of deity, instead of which she was struck from the first by what a very ordinary old woman she was, no different from so many others, just a little taller and better fed. Her face was round and her eyes as small and mobile as a child's. She was finishing chewing something and Jole deduced that she had made her wait in order to eat in peace. She was wearing dark blue clothes and her white hair was gathered behind her neck in a bun like a big onion, held in place with a hairnet.

She did not beat about the bush. "Was it you who brought that mangy little hen?" she asked.

"Yes," Jole replied in embarrassment. At home, she thought, they would have got enough eggs from the hen to last months, and enough meat for three meals.

"What's your problem?" the Holy Woman asked.

Jole took off her hat and gave a little bow. "It's my brother," she said, pointing to him. "He's the reason I came."

The woman looked over at him. He appeared to have got worse again. His body had once more started shaking and he seemed to be in the grip of a deep delirium.

"Can you bring him in here?" the Holy Woman asked.

63

"I'll try."

Jole put an arm under his neck and laboriously lifted him and carried him into the room, which was in semi-darkness, lit only by two candles placed at the sides.

There was a lingering blanket of incense in the air, with a smell like the one Jole remembered from years earlier from the old monastery in Campese and the church in Asiago. Strange, disturbing objects of worship were strewn willy-nilly about every corner of the room: rosaries hanging on the walls, sacred images of saints and madonnas which in the gloom, rather than offering comfort, instilled even more fear.

"Lay him down here!" the Holy Woman said, indicating a low, unmade camp bed, beneath a window whose heavy curtains blocked the light. Then she moved closer to the boy, holding a candle. "What happened to him?"

"He has a high fever, convulsions, he's delirious…"

The woman looked carefully at Sergio's face and hands, lifted his jumper and shirt and checked his chest, then started touching his neck and forehead. Seeing the red spots on his arms, a look of horror came over her face. She made the sign of the cross and grabbed a small glass phial from among the many on the table behind her.

"What is it?" Jole asked in alarm.

The Holy Woman abruptly silenced her with a gesture and then poured a few drops from the phial onto Sergio's chest, sprinkling the liquid with one finger and making a St Andrew's cross.

She closed her eyes and whispered a strange formula. Then she took another small phial and repeated the same gestures.

"How long has he been like this?" she suddenly asked.

"Two days now. What's wrong with him? Is it serious?"

The Holy Woman placed the palm of her right hand on the boy's stomach and kept it there. Then she looked at Jole.

"Where are you from?" she said, continuing to draw strange signs on Sergio's skin and sprinkling it with ointments and liquids that gave off strong, penetrating smells.

"Nevada."

"Does anyone up there wish you harm?"

Jole was taken aback, and the only thing she managed to say was: "I don't… I don't think so."

"Your brother is the victim of a curse. Someone has put the evil eye on him."

Jole ran her hands through her hair. "A curse?" she asked in astonishment.

"Do I have to repeat myself?" the Holy Woman replied irritably.

Jole looked at her, incapable of understanding what was happening.

"Don't worry, he'll pull though! You did the right thing coming to see me, because only I can save him."

Jole heaved a sigh of relief.

"But you have to do what I tell you."

The Holy Woman ordered Jole to dress him again, then took a bottle full of something dark and poured a few drops on Sergio's mouth. After a few seconds, he stopped shaking. Then she walked over to a cabinet full of drawers and com-partments and from one of these extracted a few handfuls of

65

herbs, which she placed inside a piece of cloth. She pulled it tight, knotted it and put it on Sergio's chest, under the shirt.

"Leave it there at least until tomorrow morning," she said.

She made the sign of the cross again, turned to the image of St Roch and muttered some words Jole did not understand. From the same cabinet she took a phial containing a thick greenish liquid and showed it to Jole.

"I've lifted the curse," she said, "but now you have to make sure he drinks this, three drops a day. Do it for three days in a row and he'll get better."

Jole looked at her, incredulous but grateful. "Are you sure?"

"He'll need to rest a little. These infusions will make him sleep. Then the fever will go away and he'll be right as rain."

"Thank you!" Jole said, hands joined. "May God bless you!"

"Now go!" the woman ordered, opening the door for her.

Jole took the miraculous phial and stuffed it in her jacket pocket, put her hat back on her head, lifted Sergio and left the room. Without that dense incense smoke she felt she could breathe again. Three people were sitting waiting their turn, a sad-looking man and two women. One was as white as a sheet and the other was holding her belly, in the grip of terrible stabbing pains. Jole and Sergio crossed the room and walked out.

"Come on, little brother. Just hold on. I was right to bring you here, wasn't I?"

19

A S SHE RODE BACK through the hamlet of Oliero, the bells of the church tolled midday. She took some dry bread and a piece of aged Asiago cheese from the pockets of her trousers and ate them slowly.

She was tired, but hoped that the journey really had been worth it. She thought again about the Holy Woman, how she had imagined her and how she really was. She thought again about that long wait, the people who were sick and had gone in ahead of them, how humiliated she had felt over the hen, one of the most valuable things the De Boers could have offered her. A curse, the Holy Woman had said. Jole wondered how this could be possible. She had become like that, no longer trusting anyone or anything. A thousand questions and doubts were bouncing about in her head, not only about the Holy Woman's honesty, but also about her rough, abrupt manner. Nor was she really convinced by those oils and ointments. Actually, they smelt of nothing more than propolis and pollen in alcohol. Not to mention the obscure, mysterious rites. Despite a slight hint of anguish, she started to feel calmer as she advanced on the cart towards the wooded crag of the Frenzela Valley that would lead her back home, since she knew she had done what she had considered necessary for Sergio. Before leaving the main road to begin the climb, she stopped for a moment, got out of the cart and went to check on him.

He was sleeping again, more peacefully now, although the skin of his face was still pale and swollen. She touched his forehead. The fever was still high. Jole sighed and was about to set off again when she heard herself being called from behind by two male voices.

"Halt!" cried the first of them.

"Stop!" called the second. "Carabinieri!"

In an instant the two men caught up with her, sitting on their slender white horses, horses such as had not been seen in these valleys for a long time.

Their uniforms were clean and new, black and shiny as a raven's plumage, with two red stripes down the sides of their trousers. On their heads they wore broad, elegant cocked hats with red and blue plumes, and their coats bristled with gold buttons, flashes and other trinkets so rich and glittery that Jole wondered if these men were really at the service of the people or only of the rich.

"Good day to you, signorina!"

"Good day to you."

They were both young and short, with neat, thin little moustaches that stood out on their olive-skinned faces.

"Where are you going?"

Jole looked at the face of the mountain above their heads, hidden in the fog and mist of a damp, dreary day.

"Home," she said. "I'm going home, up there in Nevada."

The two men exchanged sneaky smiles.

"The lair of smugglers," the first one said. "Do you know any?"

"No, I don't know any smugglers," she replied in a resolute tone.

"We need to see what you're carrying in the cart," one said, dismounting.

They spoke with very noticeable foreign accents. Clearly they were men of the South, brought here from some distant land, the kind of place Jole could not even imagine existed.

Jole took umbrage. "My brother's sleeping in the cart. Leave him alone. He's very sick."

The two men looked at each other in annoyance. The one who was still on his horse signalled to the other to lift the blankets and check what they were hiding.

"She's right, there's a young boy here," he said as soon as he saw Sergio. "And he doesn't look well."

"I told you," she said angrily.

The carabiniere covered Sergio again.

A group of people passed them, heading in the direction of the village. They were all walking slowly, with bowed heads.

The carabinieri and Jole broke off for a moment to watch them.

"The more people leave, the less trouble we'll have," one of the two men murmured.

The other laughed and turned back to Jole.

"Are you hiding something, signorina? You know we can search you."

He said this with a malevolent sneer that scared Jole. She had to get out of this situation.

"I'm not hiding anything at all, I just want to get home and put my brother to bed."

"And why did you come all the way down here?" the first man asked.

"There's a woman in the village they all call the Holy Woman."

The two men looked at each other as if weighing up what to do. After a few moments the first man looked Jole in the eyes and said:

"If you do find out anything about the smugglers, don't hesitate to report it to the barracks. These people are cunning and anti-patriotic, contemptible men who plot against the future of Italy!"

"And remember," the second man threatened, "we have the power to do what we want to you, when we want. Understood, signorina?" He got back on his horse.

Jole nodded, speechless. In her heart she despised them, just as she despised all those who took advantage of their own positions, their own roles, to lord it over the poor instead of being on their side.

The carabinieri said goodbye to her, commanded their horses to turn and rode back down to the valley at a trot.

Jole immediately shifted her gaze to the mountain face and set off again, knowing she would get home no earlier than sunset.

She left the main road, crossed the river, started along the stone path that led into a forest of hazelnut and *aier*, the Alpine maples so common in these parts, and began to climb, her head filled with thoughts. The only sound was that of the four wooden wheels, as they creaked and bounced over the pebbles along the path. A constant, continuous sound that became quite hypnotic.

She wondered how her father would greet her, how long it would take Sergio to get well again. Above all she thought about her life, now and in the future.

She felt in her chest an unexpressed sentiment of gentleness and femininity, mixed with an anger and a frustration she couldn't tame, a sense of exhaustion, a desire for revenge. And anxiety, a great deal of anxiety, despair at feeling like a failure, incapable of escaping a world that had nothing to offer her but toil, sacrifice and misery. And together with all this, she was aware of the savagery that had been festering inside her for the last two years, ready to burst out suddenly like a wolf pouncing on its prey and plunging its teeth into its neck. Yet despite everything, she felt that she must not abandon the hope of finding peace. An inner peace such as she had not known for a long time.

Where this peace was, though, where it was hiding, she could not work out.

Of this Jole was thinking as she climbed to higher ground and rode through a thick forest of ash, chestnut and hackberry, which would soon give way to conifers. Confused and restless thoughts went through her head while the world around her grew increasingly dark, though the mist and clouds were slowly yielding to the broad sky of evening.

The first nightingales began to sing.

Samson climbed the slope unperturbed, dragging behind him Jole, Sergio and their misfortune.

At that very moment, just a few dozen metres from them, Ruggero and Strim were on their way back down to the valley, hidden in the dense forest, elusive as a pair of golden jackals.

20

IN THE CONVENT of San Girolamo in Bassano, the Augustinian nuns had only just finished the services and rites of perpetual adoration. They had genuflected in unison, formed two well-ordered files and, heads bowed, left the chapel of the Sacred Heart where they had contemplated the Holy Sacrament, alternating silence and prayers.

Walking slowly and singing hymns together with her sisters, Antonia was overflowing with joy, as though within these high, strong old walls she had at last found an inner fulfilment.

Preceded by the mistress of ceremonies, they advanced together to the refectory, singing the *Magnificat*.

> *Magnificat*
> *anima mea Dominum,*
> *et exultavit spiritus meus*
> *in Deo salutari meo*
> *quia respexit humilitatem ancillae suae:*
> *ecce enim ex hoc beatam me dicent omnes generationes.*

Antonia walked with the others, bringing up the rear beside a fellow novice.

Quia fecit mihi magna qui potens est,
et Sanctum nomen eius
et misericordia eius a progenie in progenies
timentibus eum.
Fecit potentiam in brachio suo:
dispersit superbos mente cordis sui
deposuit potentes de sede,
et exaltavit humiles.

She sang with joy, even though she did not know Latin and had learnt the prayers by heart as an endless song. She listened to the voices combining to become a single deep voice and echoing between the walls of the church, the cloister and the guest quarters.

Esurientes implevit bonis,
et divites dimisit inanes.
Suscepit Israel, puerum suum,
recordatus misericordiae suae
sicut locutus est ad patres nostros,
Abraham et semini eius in saecula...

A sudden thought flashed into her head, distracting her from the prayer. As they walked down the long corridor that led from the chapter house to the refectory, she raised her eyes and, without being seen by the others, glanced towards one of the many windows that looked out on the large cloister. Just then, a raven landed on the sill, right in front of her eyes, and began pecking at the glass with its strong beak.

Antonia shuddered, immediately took her eyes away and continued singing and looking down at the ancient floor, where her feet advanced one after the other at a regular pace.

Once in the refectory, the nuns took their places at the two long tables, while one of the sisters went to the lectern to continue the prayers.

"*Santa Maria Mater Dei*," the nun chanted in a solemn tone and a voice that echoed between the high walls of the refectory. "*Libera nos a malo!* Deliver us from evil!" and so saying, she raised her arms to heaven.

"*Libera nos a malo!*" they all responded in unison.

While the others sat down, the sister at the lectern continued:

> *Tota pulchra es Maria.*
> *Et macula originalis non est in Te*
> *Tu gloria Ierusalem.*
> *Tu laetitia Israel.*
> *Tu honorificentia populi nostri.*
> *Tu advocata peccatorum.*
> *O Maria, o Maria.*
> *Virgo prudentissima,*
> *Mater clementissima.*
> *Ora pro nobis.*
> *Intercede pro nobis.*
> *Ad Dominum Iesum Christum*
> *Amen*

"Amen!" the others responded. And they began to dine in silence, while Antonia continued thinking about that raven. In her head the words "*Libera nos a malo*" continued to toll like a bell.

21

B Y THE TIME JOLE was nearing Nevada, the sun had already
set. The air was cold and damp and Sergio was asleep
in the cart, lying beneath three layers of cloths and blankets.

Jole finally passed the hill beyond which were the meadows
and the De Boers' house.

The clouds had risen like steam, forming a layer of high
cumulus that covered the whole sky, obscuring the full moon
but letting a small glimmer of light peer through.

Jole glimpsed her house. She turned to look at her brother
and saw him move. She heaved a sigh of relief.

Samson was not tired, and yet the closer he drew to his goal
the more signs of nervousness he displayed, so much so that
Jole was forced to pull hard on the reins to calm him down
and force him to proceed calmly to his destination.

When she reached the dark yard in front of the *meléster*, she
got out of the cart and went to Sergio, surprised that neither
her mother nor her father had come running out to greet her.

Samson began to neigh and paw at the ground with his
front hooves for no apparent reason.

"Quiet now!" Jole cried.

She slipped off the blankets covering her brother and
looked at him. He was better. It seemed to her that the fever
had dropped, although he had soiled himself during the ride.

"Papà! Mamma!" she called out. "We're back!"

She loaded Sergio on her back and carried him to the front door. It was open.

"We're home, little brother," she whispered in his ear. She went inside, panting. The house was dark and cold.

"They must have gone down to look for us!" she said out loud.

They would have closed the door, she thought a second later.

She called to her parents again. Groping in the darkness, she carried Sergio to his room and laid him temporarily on the floor. Then she went to the kitchen, blew on the embers still burning in the stove, revived the fire with a few small pieces of wood, put a big log over them and lit some candles around the house. She went back to her brother, washed him, changed him and put him to bed, drawing the blankets over him.

Sergio had stopped shaking and even the swelling seemed to have gone down.

"Hey!" she said. "Sergio!"

He slowly opened his eyes.

Jole took from her pocket the syrup the Holy Woman had given her and poured a little into his mouth, although she overdid it and almost risked choking him. At this point, he roused himself for a moment.

"Sleep now. I'll be back in a minute."

She left the room and resumed her search for her parents.

"Mamma! Papà! Where are you?"

Where can they have gone?

Samson was still pawing the ground and the lugubrious cries of owls began to ring out, insistent and mysterious. There were long-eared owls, little owls and tawny owls and their calls were joined by the howling of wolves. The howling was disquieting and it seemed to Jole to be coming ever closer.

A strange presentiment went through her heart, fleet as a fox. She ran to the kitchen stove and stoked the fire with more pieces of beech, then lit a big candle, put on a heavier jacket and went out to see what was causing the uproar from the animals.

Although compact, the fluffy clouds were thinning out, illumined by the light of the moon, which was struggling to show itself to the world.

Jole looked around, her heart throbbing with anxiety.

She decided to walk around the outside of the house to try to work out where her parents might have gone, and check that everything was all right. She went quickly, as far as the hen coop, without noticing anything strange.

All that remained was the shed. After a few steps, though, she stumbled over something big and fell to the ground in the mud. The candle went out immediately and Jole hurt her wrist. While she was getting back on her feet, the big full moon managed at last to break though the wall of clouds.

From it there descended a great pale light that spilt over the whole area around Nevada. In an instant, the landscape, from the wooded hills to the distant mountains, from the pastures on higher ground to the meadows around the De Boers' house, was lit with the evanescent, soft, milky light coming from the sky. It was as if the night had opened its eyes all at once, awakening from a dream. Jole opened hers, too, and saw what she would never have wanted to see. The obstacle over which she had stumbled was her mother's body.

Jole leapt to her feet and rushed to her mother, incredulous. She was lying on her stomach, with one cheek sunk in the mud. She had been stabbed in the back and her eyes were wide open.

At the sight, Jole felt the blood freeze in her veins. She had the sudden terrifying sensation that she was living through a nightmare. Her arms and legs trembling in panic, she gently took hold of the upper part of her mother's body and turned it over. A trickle of blood emerged from Agnese's mouth, but she was still breathing.

"Mamma!" Jole cried in a heartrending voice.

The animals of the forest immediately fell silent, as if the mountain and its creatures, the plants, the tallest trees and the wind that blew up there were respectfully rapt and attentive when faced with Jole's grief. All was quiet, as if sunk in a deep sleep, while the rays of the moon softened the lined and suffering features of Agnese's face.

"Mamma!" Jole repeated, raising her mother's head.

There was still a small, weak breath in Agnese's body, stubbornly held in reserve so that she could tell her daughter something.

"Jole…" she sighed almost imperceptibly.

Jole came close to her lips.

"They took it all away…"

Jole burst into tears. She thought she might die. She wished she could take her mother's place, she could not come to terms with this situation, she did not understand a thing, she was confused.

79

"Who was it? Who was it?" she kept asking, her tears falling on Agnese's cheeks and mingling with her blood.

"A man with a face like a monster… And a fat man…"

Jole listened without understanding.

"He tried to stop them… They killed him…" she managed to add, turning her eyes towards the path that led to the *masiere*.

And with these words Agnese breathed her last and her soul went out of her.

The echo of Jole's desperate scream resounded through the mountains.

Collapsing onto her mother's body, she fell into despair. She was incapable of getting back on her feet or trying to understand.

Some fifty metres away from them, over towards the tobacco terraces, lay the corpse of Augusto, that strong, resolute man, that enduring father who had spent a lifetime raising his children, breaking his back to feed them every day. He lay beneath the pitiless gaze of a moon that, like a coward, exposed every detail of the pain he had felt in both living and dying.

He lay on his back beside one of his hiding places, a pitchfork stuck in his belly.

22

T HE FEW CLOUDS LEFT in the sky gradually vanished as if to step aside from that scene of grief.

They faded away out of respect and compassion for a young woman who had been torn apart, left suddenly alone without the pillars that had supported her life, her past and her present. Over her father's body Jole wept a lifetime's tears, because in that interminable weeping there was not only the pain of a daughter, but also the sense of guilt and the grief over an unbearable loss.

Together with the mountains, her parents had given her everything.

Especially her father.

Forgive me if lately I often quarrelled with you. You taught me about day and night, about the woods, the animals, and the wind…

And she cried uninterruptedly.

Kneeling in the mud by her parents' bodies, she wondered if she could have avoided this tragedy by remaining here instead of going down to see the Holy Woman. She had disobeyed her father and now she found herself like this, with nothing. Without her parents, to whom she had not listened. The weight she felt in her chest turned to weeping and infinite despair.

She tried to get up, swayed, fell.

What can I do now? All I want is to let myself die here, beside you. To let time cover me and my face become earth. It's my fault, only my fault. I should have listened to my Papà...

She tried again to get up, but her legs gave way and again she fell to the ground, her face in the mud, in the grip of convulsions.

Then she lost consciousness.

23

J OLE KNEW VERY WELL that there are times in life when
everything may collapse around us.

She also knew that it can happen suddenly, perhaps just
when we are not thinking of life's difficulties, or worse, when
we think we are really strong and are certain we have our feet
firmly planted on the ground. And then, when everything col-
lapses around us, we remain on our feet almost miraculously,
perhaps balancing on our toes, although we have no idea how
we will be able to maintain that balance.

But something even worse can happen, and this, too, Jole
knew. It may be that not only does what is around us collapse,
but that we collapse as well. Not because we are incapable
of keeping our balance for a long time – like a chamois on
the slender ridge of a crag – on that thin, fragile borderline
between good and evil, between reason and madness, life and
death. But because when the landslide comes it may sweep us
away, without giving us time to clutch a rocky spur.

And then, inevitably, we plummet, and in plummeting we no
longer see anything, we find ourselves in a dark, blind flight that
makes us lose the taste and scent of things. The air is different,
stifling, and the sky low and dark, and our breathing becomes
ever more laboured. At that moment everything changes. The
meaning we give to our existence changes. Everything loses

colour at that moment, vanishes into an unavoidable, tragic umbra. Of course Jole knew these things.

All this happens because we ourselves are that landslide, we become that collapse. And then, but only after we have smashed to the ground, we become aware, through a sixth sense, of the true meaning of things, their most private and precious value. We become aware of what life really means to tell us, even if by now it is too late. And we smile at what was good and regret the good we did not do. That is the moment, a brief, fleeting moment outside physical time, in which we realize that losing everything has a meaning only if first we have left a sign that remains. A sign that binds our passage, with courage and loyalty, to the passage of the people dearest to us. And then we realize the absolute importance of the pacts respected, the promises kept even over a period of years, the loyalty of a word given. Loyalty and justice.

These, Jole understood, are the things that matter. These are the values for which we come into the world. This, only this matters, if we have grasped its importance and have pursued its ultimate meaning with determination. Only in this way can we calmly agree to collapse, and then be able to pick ourselves up again. Because only in this case can we hear a voice. And that voice, Jole thought, must be listened to. Because it is a sound that does not reach our ears from somewhere else, but from inside us. It is a voice that never shouts, but whispers, like a distant breeze, and to hear it we have to be silent and still, and above all want to hear it. We have to want it.

And deep in her heart Jole wanted it, that voice of eternal loyalty. She needed it to survive, to get back on her feet, remove the rubble from her back and look at the dawn that would arrive after that accursed full moon. She wanted that voice. Precisely because her father and mother had taught her never to give up, always to look ahead. And they had also taught her indirectly that, out of a sense of justice with respect to their lives of toil and sacrifice, she would have to redeem them in some way. She would have to make them live again for ever.

Collapsing, listening to the voice, getting up again.

24

JOLE CAME BACK TO LIFE and slowly opened her eyes, which were filled with tears and mud.

Everything seemed out of focus, but blurred as her vision was, she heard that voice. Oh, yes, she heard it.

Around her the first light of dawn was pouring down.

The air, until that moment as still and stagnant as a mountain puddle, began slowly, inexplicably, to move, bringing a breath of cold, healthy wind that dried the tears on her face and stirred her long hair. The wind picked up, and alongside its sibilant murmur the sounds of the forest also began to be heard again. Animal cries echoed, treetops and branches rustled. The breath from the north was rousing her, calling her as a father calls a daughter. She recognized it immediately. It was the wind from the border, the wind she had known before. It had come to pity her and raise her up, to command her to keep going. It was the same wind that blew over the borders between weakness and strength, cowardice and bravery, humiliation and redemption.

Jole rose to her knees and got back on her feet. Her hair loose, she gathered her hat from the ground and struck it twice to rid it of the wet earth. Nature and the mountains – this she felt now – were and would always be on her side. Fate had wanted her to survive. And that was enough for her to decide what she had to achieve.

Peace for her dear ones. Justice for her.

25

NEVADA WAS DESERTED. There was not a soul about for kilometres.

I'll never ever call the carabinieri. And I don't want a priest either. Where would I go to find one anyway? All the way to Foza? Or else down into the valley? No. That's not what I have to do.

She listened again to the wind flooding the plateau and the surrounding valleys with its cold, deep voice, while the first rays of a sun still hidden behind the mountains began to disperse the night's breath from the meadows.

She put a hand on her heart and told herself she had to get by alone, alone and with the mountains. She decided that Augusto and Agnese would remain here, in their home, in the earth where they had always lived, amid these mountains, watched over by these woods. It was only right that they should hear the sound of that wind for all eternity, since it was the most sacred, most spiritual thing she could offer them and their memory.

Summoning her strength, she went back to the house and gathered a pickaxe, a shovel, two small planks of wood, a hammer and some nails.

She put them in a sack, loaded it on her back and returned to where her parents lay. In the dawn light she looked around and found the right spot, on the little hill at the edge of the larch wood. Because larches were the favourite trees of both and because those magical trees, with their inimitable beauty, would every day reflect that place of light and colour, honouring them better than a few picked flowers laid in a grey cemetery.

With her last remaining energy, her eyes starting to flow once more with unquenchable tears, she dug a big, deep hole and placed both bodies in it.

The pain was unbearable. She covered them with earth and over the mound that had formed planted a wooden cross, a touch lopsided but solidly fixed.

One cross for the two of them. And no inscription.

"Peace!" Jole whispered. "May God bless you."

The rising sun saw everything. The woods saw everything.

The mountains and the solitary wind not only saw, but suffered with her.

And blessed for ever that night and that earth.

A quiver ran through the wood behind her. The ground, the branches, the sky all shook.

Like a rebirth. A genesis.

26

S HE LINGERED, staring sadly at the grave that she herself
had dug.

She had no more tears, no more voice, no more strength. It
was cold, but she did not feel it. She did not feel anything at all.

She turned to look at the house. She could not believe that
she would never again see them within those walls. Only Sergio
was left to her now. Thinking of her little brother warmed
her heart. The boy needed her. She was the only person he
could count on.

What will I say to him? she thought. *How can I tell him what
happened?*

She gathered the shovel and the pickaxe and trudged home
in the light of a sun that would not hear of abandoning her
on the earth.

At the door she dropped everything, went in, and with
mud- and bloodstained hands rekindled the stove. She went
to the sump where they kept the cold water brought up from
the river and washed her face and hands.

Her brother was asleep. He seemed better: his face was less
drawn and his brow no longer burning hot. Jole was agitated,
her heart pounding. Suddenly she remembered that, when her
mother was very agitated, she would drink a special infusion
that made her feel better.

She went to the old applewood sideboard, located the tin box she was looking for, took out two small copper containers filled with intense-smelling hemp leaves and made herself an infusion in the small saucepan on the stove. When it was ready she started sipping it calmly. Gradually her body warmed up and her limbs relaxed. The confusion and anxiety faded, and at last she fell into a deep, soothing sleep.

Agnese had always said that hemp was the only remedy when she was agitated. Augusto had bartered tobacco for a little of it every year, down in the valley. Because whereas tobacco grew well on the right bank of the Brenta, the left was ideal for hemp.

27

S ERGIO WAS HAVING beautiful, exquisite dreams.
He was aware that he was dreaming, but he hoped he
would not wake up again.

Patches of bright, vivid colours alternated in his mind,
mingled and overlapped, producing sublime sounds and music.

All at once these masses of colour formed shapes, and
Sergio found himself in the midst of a luxuriant forest full of
exotic trees and plants laden with ripe, opulent fruit of a kind
he had never seen in his life. The trees were so tall it seemed
they would never end, and might reach heaven. Milk and
honey gushed from their trunks.

Sergio approached one of the trees to get a closer look at
its miraculous bark, and all of a sudden his parents emerged
from its sap. They were young and handsome. They began to
stroll through that magical forest, holding hands.

He called to them, but they did not hear him.

He watched them happily as they walked away, and he
went back to the tree to taste the honey and the milk flowing
from it. But as soon as he put his mouth to it, the dream faded.

He, though, continued to sleep.

28

B Y THE TIME JOLE WOKE, the sun had been up for several hours.

She opened her heavy, swollen eyes. Everything looked murky. She was lying on the floor of the kitchen. The stove was still warm. In an instant she remembered everything and a terrible anxiety gripped her. She hoped it had all been a dream, but when she did not hear the voices of her family around her she realized that it had really happened, and she closed her eyes again and wept. She did not know if she would be able to face that day, or the following day, or any of the days to come.

She got laboriously to her feet, dragged herself to the front door and forced herself to look up towards the little hill beneath the larches. She hoped not to see that mound of fresh earth or the wooden cross. But there they were. It was all true. The strong morning sun bore witness to it, cruelly, cynically.

She came back in and went to her brother's room. He was still asleep. She ran her hand through his hair.

I don't know how or when to tell you, she thought.

"Sergio…" she said softly. "Wake up, Sergio…"

The boy moved his dry, cracked lips and lifted an eyelid.

Jole ran to get water from the kitchen and brought it to him.

He took two little sips, but could not manage to say anything.

Jole looked at him, her heart breaking.

He put his head back down on the pillow and lay for while with his eyes open, staring up at the old dark beams on the ceiling.

She stroked him again.

Sergio could not keep his eyes open, nor move, so debilitated was he after three days of high fever.

Jole gave him two spoonfuls of broth, left the house with a sick feeling in her stomach and looked at the surrounding landscape. For the first time in her life, the sun of home appeared strange to her. That sun marked the beginning of a new existence, as if from that moment, that morning, a new course was beginning for her. A whole other life.

She went around the outside of the house, imagining that round every corner her father or her mother would reappear and give her a big hug.

She went back to the places where she had found their bodies. There were many traces of blood scattered here and there, and in the mud – especially close to where she had discovered her father – horses' hoof-marks and many signs of struggle, testimony to the fact that her father had tried as best he could to resist the barbaric attack.

Then something drew Jole's attention.

She examined the ground more carefully and in at least four or five spots, with quite some distance between them, she noticed something that made her retch. Tracks. Or rather, prints. Some were of her father's boots. She recognized them immediately.

The others were of two kinds, and it was clear that they belonged to two men. Many were quite distinct, pressed deep into the mud and earth.

Jole did not want to believe it. Her heart leapt into her throat. She took a deep breath, then bent down to get a closer look: big pointed boots. She ran to the hiding places from which her father's last eight ingots had been stolen. And there, too, she noticed the same prints. Big pointed boots. They were definitely his, she was sure of it, since she had never before seen boots made in that way or prints of that kind. Not far away, in the mud, she spotted a piece of fabric. She looked at it closely: a large grey kerchief.

"The bastards!" she said, her voice full of venom.

It was as if that new sun had suddenly revealed everything to her and was promising her its support: it would always be on her side, and from that moment on would light her way.

A man with a face like a monster... And a fat man... It was only now that Jole recalled her mother's last words. Words, like the prints, that pointed the finger at those two.

Her hands were trembling like birch leaves in autumn. But not from weakness. Rather, it was a sign that an unstoppable force was rising deep inside her. It was the force of that proud, wild instinct that Jole had not felt since the days of her journey across the border.

She clenched her fists, ran back inside the house and carried out everything they held dearest. There were not many things, but they were important: some objects and souvenirs her mother had kept in the drawer next to her oakwood bed, two images of the Virgin and a crucifix hanging on the wall that she had always prayed to with great devotion, some of Sergio's clothes and a few of his carved wooden playthings. Toy horses, above all.

She decided that she was tired of her old hat. From this day on, she would wear her father's hat, which was even wider and had a larger brim.

She grabbed all the available food in the sideboard: speck, eggs, sausage, aged Asiago cheese, Morlacco and Bastardo. Hard, old black bread. She loaded everything on the cart, cloths and blankets included, and with great excitement harnessed Samson.

She went back inside and tried to wake Sergio.

"We're leaving, little brother!"

He lifted his head slightly.

"Antonia will take care of you for a few days. I'm taking you down to her."

She took him in her arms and laboriously propped him up in the bed of the cart.

She rushed into the shed, went straight to a corner and climbed up into a kind of loft that Augusto had constructed the previous year.

With the help of a pickaxe she prised up two of the floorboards. Her eyes, which had changed for ever, lit up with a wild, arcane light. Because under those floorboards she found the two rifles from their old adventure. She recognized them: Augusto's St Peter and her own St Paul.

She looked at the two Werndl-Holubs for a few moments, undecided.

For you, Papà!

She took St Peter and all the remaining cartridges, climbed down from the loft, left the shed and bolted the door.

I remember how well it loosens tongues!

She hid the rifle in a long holster her horse carried against his abdomen.

From a drawer she took the pendant her sister had made for her, the dandelion embedded in resin. Putting it around her neck, she felt stronger.

She threw in the stove the phial she had been given by the Holy Woman, cursing her as she did so.

She closed the front door behind her and climbed onto the cart.

She took one last glance at the little hill where her parents were buried.

Peace to them and justice for all, she thought, her stomach contorted with pain.

Then she lifted the reins and cried:

"Ya!"

Samson's muscles vibrated and the wheels of the cart creaked. Very slowly, they began to move over the mud and earth.

It was a late morning in mid-November. The air was thin and cold, and the sky was clear. Jole felt weak, but sure of what she was doing.

Because if the previous night she had been afraid of losing her own past, now she realized that in a way it had come back to her. She touched the big hat she was wearing on her head and felt all her father's determination and perseverance fall on her.

All at once, a strong wind rose, blowing down towards the valley, wanting to show her the way and drive her towards her destiny.

Jole recognized that wind and knew that two more voices would be joining its voice.

She closed her eyes and listened to the powerful, poetic sound.

And, smiling, she crossed the meadow and set off down the slope that would take her back to the valley.

29

S HE QUICKLY DESCENDED, passing between the forests and hugging the rock faces that fell sheer to the Brenta Valley.

Every now and again Sergio would raise his head, peer out from the blankets and look around in confusion.

He felt exhausted, with not even the strength to speak. He looked at his white hands, which had grown thinner and were shaking. As the cart made its way down, Sergio wondered where his mother and father were, but his head felt heavy and he could not think about anything. He would lie down and cover himself again, abandoning himself to the constant jolts of the cart.

Reaching the bank of the great river, Jole turned and headed south. She rode through Solagna and Campese and eventually came to Bassano del Grappa.

Arriving at last at the convent of San Girolamo, she commanded the horse to stop.

She dismounted and walked up to the big wooden door of the convent.

She pounded on it three times and, after a few seconds, another four times.

A small hole opened up in it, and from it a nun's calm, reassuring voice emerged.

"Jesus Christ be praised."

"May He ever be praised," Jole replied.

"Who is knocking at the convent door?"

"My name is Jole De Boer. I come from the mountains of Nevada, and I'm here to speak to my sister Antonia, who's a novice with you."

"It's me!" The heavy door opened.

"Antonia!" Jole cried, throwing her arms around her sister and hugging her tight.

"How lovely to see you again, Jole! What on earth brings you here? Why are you wearing Papà's hat?"

Jole did not let go. Antonia looked at the cart behind her sister. From beneath the blankets the head of her little brother emerged.

"Sergio!" Antonia said. "How lovely to see both of you!"

Then she noticed something unusual about her sister's manner: she was strangely taciturn. She also became aware that Sergio, usually as agile and swift as a marmot and highly talkative, was unable to rise and get down off the cart. Nor did he say a word.

He waved at her and again fell asleep, despite the kisses and caresses of his sister, whom he had not seen for months and months.

Antonia took Jole by the shoulders and looked her in the eyes. She was thin and emaciated, her cheeks hollow and her expression numb.

"Sister, what happened? How are Mamma and Papà?"

"You have to do me a great favour," Jole said.

"How are they? And what about you two? Why are you in this state?"

"First promise me something, in the name of God."

"Go ahead."

"You have to take care of Sergio for a while. He's ill. I need to go away."

"What's wrong with him? And where do you have to go?"

"Three days ago he went to Campomulo in search of mountain pine, and since then he's had convulsions and a high fever. You'll be able to look after him here."

"I'll take him to see the sister apothecary, don't worry. Though I'll have to ask permission of the mother superior first. Where do you have to go?"

"The mother superior will allow it, of course she will. He's your brother, and he's a child, isn't he? But I don't know where I'm going."

"What are you saying, Jole?"

Without waiting for a reply, Antonia called one of the nuns and asked her to take the boy to the infirmary. The nun immediately took him carefully in her arms and went inside the convent with him.

"Jole," Antonia said, "this is all very strange. Tell me what happened and where you're going!"

"I have to find out what happened to Mamma and Papà," Jole said in a low voice, then burst into tears.

"For the love of God, what are you hiding from me?"

"Antonia, promise me you'll keep it secret from Sergio."

"What happened, sister?" She raised her hands to her chest and her eyes grew watery. "Don't tell me…"

"They're both dead."

Feeling faint, Antonia leant against the door, then made the sign of the cross and burst into tears, clinging to Jole.

They stood like this for a few minutes, until another nun came to demand an explanation.

The mother superior, having been informed and moved to pity, allowed Jole to bring the cart into the outer courtyard of the convent and spend a little time with Antonia.

Jole and Antonia went to the large cloister. They sat there for a few minutes in silence, while the song of the birds alternated with that of the bells.

Jole told her everything, except that she had buried their parents close to home, in their mountains.

She also told her that Sergio, still in the grip of that damned fever, knew nothing about it.

"And for now it's best you don't tell him, all right?" she added.

Antonia nodded, slow and pensive, and murmured:

"Killed for money after a life of sacrifice… Greed turns men into beasts."

Jole put a hand on her shoulder.

"When did it happen?" Antonia asked desperately. "Why didn't you let me know about the funeral? How could you do this to me?"

"The priest in Foza did everything in a hurry."

"May God welcome Mamma and Papà with mercy. But what about the law? Have the carabinieri been informed? Who's looking for these murderers?"

"I'm sure they'll be caught soon."

Antonia looked at her suspiciously. "I know you – don't do

anything crazy! Revenge serves no purpose. And I beg you, don't turn wicked."

"I'm not wicked. It's life that makes people wicked, Antonia."

"Do you want to replace divine justice? Do you want to prove to yourself how brave you are?"

Jole put a hand under Antonia's chin, lifted it and looked her in the eyes with a tranquil, serene expression. "My sister," she said softly, "it doesn't take any bravery to do something that can't be avoided."

"Jole…" Antonia sighed, unable to convince her. She started crying again.

Two tears also ran down Jole's face. After a few moments' silence, she said:

"Their most precious belongings are in the cart. They don't amount to much, but I want to donate them to the convent, and the cart, too… I must go now. Take care of Sergio. I'll be back for him as soon as possible."

"Sister, I beg you," Antonia said, seizing her arm.

As gently as she could, Jole pulled away from her. She stood up and together they walked to the cart.

They held each other tightly and for a long time, as if these embraces could never be enough for them.

Jole detached Samson from the cart, mounted him and said to Antonia:

"Pray for Mamma and Papà, and for Sergio. And if you have any time left over, pray for me, too."

Antonia nodded and blessed her with a broad gesture of her arms.

Jole put a hand inside her jacket and took out the dandelion pendant. "Do you remember this?" she said, trying to smile, but not succeeding.

Antonia was moved to see the amulet. "Of course I remember it," she replied. "'Dandelion' is still your name, isn't it?"

"You know I don't like borders. I like horizons!"

And with that she urged Samson to set off.

PART TWO

1

GALLOPING ON HER HAFLINGER, she soon reached the hamlet of Oliero. She rode to the Holy Woman's house, filled with tears and anger. Before dismounting, she peered at the back, where she remembered having seen the stable with two horses. The wooden fencing was wide open and the enclosure was empty. Those two bastards might have got away.

She went back to the front of the house, leapt down and tied Samson to the iron rings fixed to the wall for the purpose. She looked around and saw there was nobody about. She opened the holster on her horse's belly and took out St Peter. She loaded it and knocked violently on the door several times.

It was opened by the same woman, who this time found herself looking into the barrel of a rifle.

"The Holy Woman's son and his crony!" Jole growled. "Where are they?"

The woman stood rooted to the spot with fear. She raised her hands in surrender and leant with one shoulder on the door frame.

"I… I don't know…" she stammered.

"Let me in!"

The woman took two steps back and stood aside.

Jole entered, holding the rifle high, and kicked the door closed behind her.

In the waiting room a few people sat hoping to see the Holy Woman. At the sight of Jole and her rifle they all took fright.

"Tell me where those two are!" she repeated to the woman. "Ruggero and… Strim. Is that right? Are those their names?"

"Yes, yes," the woman said, still holding her hands up. "Please, I beg you, don't hurt me. I really don't know where they are. They come and go. They're a pair of crooks. I haven't seen them since yesterday morning."

"Is that the truth? They're not in the house?"

"I swear! Please don't hurt me!"

Jole looked at her closely, trying to tell if she was lying. Then, heedless of the others' presence, she strode across the little room to the Holy Woman's door.

"Is someone in there?" she asked the people waiting.

One, a little old man, his cheeks and the tip of his nose as red as ripe raspberries, shook his head.

"I'll be quick," Jole said.

None of them had the courage to say a single word or even look at her, such was the fear that her expression instilled in them.

She shoved open the door, walked into the smoke-filled room and lifted the barrel of her rifle in search of the Holy Woman's face.

"Where is your son hiding?" she cried as soon as she spotted her fiddling with her phials of infusions.

"What?" the Holy Woman exclaimed in astonishment. "Who told you to come in here like this? Put down that rifle or I'll call the carabinieri. I never promised you the boy would get better."

"Call anyone and I'll shoot! I'm not here because of my brother. I'm here for that bastard, your son. You'll tell me where he's hiding if you know what's good for you!"

The Holy Woman made a strange sign of the cross, such as Jole had never seen in her life, and closed her eyes. She seemed to be praying under her breath.

"Tell me where he is!" Jole cried in a tone that betrayed her desperation. To give more emphasis to her words she went up to the woman and aimed the rifle between her eyes. "He and his crony killed my mother and father! Now that you know that, do you still want to call the carabinieri?"

The Holy Woman started sobbing. "Ru– Ruggero? Im– impossible. You're crazy!" She grabbed a phial from among the many behind her and swallowed the contents.

"You know what I'm talking about. They came up to my village and robbed and killed my parents, like wild animals. I know it was the two of them. Tell me where I can find them. Come on!"

The Holy Woman opened her eyes wide and got to her knees, as if the world had suddenly come crashing down on her. As if in a moment she had felt all the weight of an old, unbearable burden and, with it, a sense of total failure.

"I was hoping they'd never do anything bad, but—"

"But you were wrong. Which is strange, because a Holy Woman should know everything, shouldn't she? Someone who calls herself that and steals money from poor people should know everything, right?" There was contempt in Jole's voice.

"Have pity on me, girl, don't hurt me, I—"

"Tell me where he is!" Jole insisted, the rifle still trained on her.

"I confess I don't know. You have to believe me."

"Well, I don't. A mother always protects her son, even when he's a bastard."

The Holy Woman began to cry. She crawled over to the altar with the sacred images of St Anthony of Padua and St Teresa of Ávila.

Jole watched her. She felt sorry for the woman, but that did not make her change her demeanour one iota.

"You know where he is!"

The woman looked up at the saints. "He doesn't live here with me," she confessed. "Every now and again he comes and stays for a while. Sometimes that other man is with him, a foreigner. I don't know what they do when they're not here... He's always caused me problems. That's why I moved here from Vas years ago."

"Where have they gone?" Jole cried.

"They came here late last night, slept, and then rode away this morning."

"And didn't they say anything?"

"Ruggero said he didn't know when they'd be back," the woman went on, desperate now.

"I don't believe you."

"It's the truth... What do you want to do to him?"

"Nothing. I just want my things back."

"You're going to your death, girl. The man who's with him, Strim, is ruthless."

"We'll see. Where did they go? Come on, you know. Are you the Holy Woman or not?"

The woman looked at Jole in silence, eyes wild and brimming with tears. "They'll kill you… They'll kill you…" she kept saying, almost as a threat.

Jole went even closer to her, placed the barrel of St Peter on her lined old brow and lifted the hammer. "I want just two things and, if you don't give them to me, I'll kill you," she said, very calmly.

In the little room outside, practically nothing of what the two women had said to each other in those two minutes had been heard, despite the raised voices and Jole's yells. In any case, it was normal for those who visited the Holy Woman to hear screams of pain, despair and madness coming from her room, so nobody had paid all that much attention to their mingled cries.

After a while the Holy Woman opened the door, put her head out and cried in a distressed tone:

"Ester! Ester! Give her back the hen, will you?"

A few moments later, the woman with the task of greeting people entered the little room holding the hen by the legs. Jole put the rifle over her shoulder, took the hen, nodded to those present and left that house of malefactors.

"They'll kill you," the Holy Woman muttered as she watched Jole go out through the front door.

Jole put away the rifle, taking care not to be seen by anyone, tied the hen's legs with hemp twine, put her in one of the big jute sacks with which Samson was caparisoned and set off again.

2

As SHE RODE BACK through the village Jole thought of what awaited her and a cold shudder ran down her spine. She was determined at all costs to track down her parents' killers, and she knew perfectly well that they would not be easy to find or overcome. But she also knew that there are moments in life that are not about making calculations or weighing the pros and cons. Moments when you just have to risk everything.

On the square in front of the church of Santo Spirito more migrants had gathered, ready to depart. Every time Jole saw them, she recognized the same expressions, the same demeanour. On the one hand they were full of hope because of the big promises that had been made to them and all the wonderful things they had heard about the Americas; on the other, they were weighed down with hunger and the sadness of being forced to abandon their homes, their land, their history, their identity.

She rode along the right bank of the Brenta as far as Carpané and there she crossed the river over the stone bridge. Once she had reached the left bank, she stopped for a moment and looked ahead and above at the steep slope of the mountain that awaited her.

She thought again about the last words spoken by the Holy Woman who, under the pressure of St Peter's iron and lead, had finally revealed to Jole that she had accidentally overheard her son conferring with his accomplice outside the stables before they got on their horses and rode away. She had heard them say that they would be heading for Monte Grappa, to a village called Cimanegra or something like that, where they needed to hide something.

Samson was thirsty, and he began to pull towards the little watercourse that meandered from the river into a side stream a few metres away. Jole dismounted and let him drink, then led him to a little meadow where, even though it was already mid-November, the grass was still quite tall.

Well hidden from the eyes of the few people who passed that way, and isolated from the houses nearby, they remained there for a few minutes, Samson feeding and Jole drinking a little water and munching a piece of *puccia* with some *sopressa* sausage, sitting on a granite rock. When it was time to set off up the mountain, she got back on Samson and rode towards the forest of alders and downy oaks that covered the foothills of the Grappa massif.

The previous day's rain had swept the clouds from the sky, now limpid and clear as only November days can be in the mountains. The belling of the stags had been over for some weeks, the nights were drawing in and the air stung the nose even by day.

The sun was going down with its usual autumnal haste and the line separating light from dark and day from night was rising inexorably on the partly rocky, partly wooded walls of the massif, leaving in semi-darkness and cold the great deep canyon that the Brenta Valley had always been and would be for all eternity.

Jole summoned her strength, aware that she would need a lot of it. She tied her hair, rubbed her hands together, resolutely seized Samson's reins and began her climb of the precipitous slope.

She should have been exhausted, in a state of shock, her heart in shreds. In the last few days she had seen and done and lived through terrible things, things that were incredibly hard for the head and soul of such a sensitive young woman to bear. Yet she did not feel any strain. It was as if the wild excitement, the adrenaline of what awaited her had deadened all pain, all weakness, all the human frailties: the body's fatigue and the spirit's dejection.

In her blood, she felt an animal-like sense that she was going back on the attack, and this feeling gave her energy and warmed her limbs.

It was early in the afternoon of 17 November 1898 when she took a path similar in every way to the one she had twice taken in the past to get to the border.

This time, though, it would be a different journey, because there would be no marked route, no clear destination. And because, unlike the border between two countries, the border between good and evil can almost never be detected with the naked eye.

And yet, like then, she would be alone on this journey, though as she climbed the slope towards Mount Grappa, she was distinctly aware of her family's strength, the obduracy of the De Boers, inside her.

Yes, Jole was sure that the souls of her mother and father would guide her to the right place, and that the instinct of a daughter torn to the depths of her being and the intuition of a mortally wounded woman would do the rest.

3

S HE MOVED FORWARD, entering a dense forest of Alpine maples, elms, ash and now almost bare oaks.

The path was so narrow that the dry, protruding branches of the trees scraped and scratched Samson's belly and Jole's face. To protect herself, Jole pulled the red kerchief even tighter around her neck and adjusted the big hat on her head.

The forest floor was slippery, covered as it was in red and yellow and brown leaves, many of them already decaying.

Advancing on her horse, she looked at the infinite number of leaves on the ground, destined to break up and be absorbed back into the forest, while as she passed others were still detaching themselves from the highest branches and fluttering gracefully down to the earth. She thought about the cycle of their life, from when they budded in spring, to the summer when they developed and grew, turning a darker green, until autumn and the moment of their death. She picked up one that had fallen on her hat and examined it. It was from a black alder: dry, with a slightly rusty colour, and yet still beautiful in its roundness, its diagonal lines, its serrated edges. She thought of how the beauty of the leaves, of every single leaf in the wood, lay in their uniqueness. Each was different from the others. Like snowflakes, none were identical.

Just like people...

She raised her eyes to the sky but saw nothing apart from rough trunks, tangled branches and drooping leaves. The mountains were really one great school, the most important of all, certainly more so than the schools in those big towns down in the plains, where you learnt things that did not help you to live a better life, only how to abuse your power over others in the quickest and most inequitable way possible. Her thoughts wandered through the painful memory of what she had just lived though. She still could not come to terms with what had happened.

Samson proceeded tirelessly, gradually climbing the slope to higher ground. Jole stopped him for a moment, dismounted and took a few steps, looking for a gap in the trees that would give her a glimpse of the valley below, which was almost dark by now. Before her rose the Asiago Plateau, gentle but imposing. Peering halfway down, she searched for Nevada, but her thoughts were immediately distracted. As she looked for the village across the great canyon she felt the agony of it all rise in her chest and climb all the way up to her throat and then to her eyes. There she was born, there she had grown, there her parents had loved her and made her what she was. There she had suffered, endured, made many sacrifices, and yet had overcome every difficulty and become strong. Thanks to her mother and father, her brother and sister. Now her family was no longer there, her sister was part of another family and God alone knew how her brother was. For the first time she doubted herself and her bold undertaking. She felt fragile, vulnerable. She was likely to meet with a terrible fate. But she had no alternative.

I have to do it, and that's it. I have no choice. First I'll do justice to my family, then I'll go away for ever.

Clenching her fists, she got back on Samson.

No sooner had she resumed her ascent than she spotted a big nutcracker perched on the branch of a hornbeam branch. It was cleaning its breast feathers, which were dark with white patches, and occasionally glossing its beak by rubbing it from one side of the branch where it sat to the other. Jole and the bird looked at each other, then the nutcracker cawed loudly in its deep, penetrating voice and flew up and away.

Jole took it as a greeting and continued to urge Samson forward.

She had heard of Cimanegra in the past and knew more or less where it might be.

She had first heard of it at home during a brief conversation between her father and Titta, an elderly Nevada man who had died when she was ten. Titta had been there a few times to barter Nostrano tobacco for a little *mozata*, a kind of speck made from ibex meat that was almost impossible to find, since only a few of the animals were still left.

Jole recalled those years when Nevada was still inhabited. There were only three or four families, but two of them were so large that the village felt like a real community, full of children running about everywhere.

"Don't call them home!" the grandparents would say to the mothers. "When they're hungry they'll come back!"

God knows how little Sergio is doing… Jole suddenly thought.

She knew she would not get to Cimanegra until the following day, since it was growing dark and both she and Samson would have to eat, drink and rest. Her aim was to camp on the little plain above before the sun set behind the Asiago Plateau. That left her only an hour and a half of daylight. She looked down at the ground and clearly made out hoof prints on the fresh earth between one patch of leaves and the next. She dismounted and took a closer look, even though the light was becoming ever dimmer. Eight sets of prints, two horses. Tracks that had preceded her along the same path. She smiled in satisfaction. Then, surrounded and enveloped by the growing song of the nightingales, she proceeded rapidly, climbing metre by metre through a wood that had by now turned into a conifer forest.

4

AN HOUR LATER she reached the high plain at an altitude of just over a thousand metres on the south-western slope of Mount Grappa.

It covered quite an extensive area. From it, to the west, beyond the great canyon of the Brenta Valley, you could see a great deal of pastureland on the plateau, especially the plain of Marcesina.

The sun had almost set, and Jole had to move. She saw a spot sheltered by a chalky crag, close to a little spring. It was ideal: her back would be covered and she would have all the water she needed.

She dismounted, relieved her faithful travelling companion of his heavy burden of filled bags and pouches and left him to drink and graze freely. She had to light a fire and make a shelter from sticks, cloths, blankets and hemp twine.

She took a large knife from one of the bags Samson had carried and entered the wood, returning first with a decent supply of thin twigs for firewood and immediately after that with another bundle of bigger, heavier branches. The third time, though, she returned with ten or so long, solid branches perfect for building the framework of the tent. She walked over to one side of the open space and looked around for the best place to set up her shelter.

It was then that she saw them.

First one, then the other. Both in the meadow in front of her. The first was to her left, looking at her fixedly and grinding its teeth, advancing step after step towards her with an aggressive demeanour; the second stood motionless, to her right, watching her cautiously, as if calmly awaiting its moment.

Caught by surprise, Jole froze with fear, knowing that these two wolves could not possibly be alone and knowing equally well that, without a rifle in your hand, there are few chances of escape when you are faced with a pack of hungry predators.

She had always been told that in such situations it was best to keep calm: running away would only provoke them more. She took a deep breath, even though her hands had turned to ice and her heart was beating like a drum that echoed in her ears. She heard growls and, looking about her, saw four more wolves. They were approaching her from every direction, surrounding her ever more closely. One of them suddenly began to howl, confidently, as if alerting others of its kind in the distance. Jole dropped the branches she had been holding and tried to collect her thoughts. The rifle was eight paces away from her. In the meantime, the number of wolves, ever closer and more threatening, had increased to nine. They were thin and mangy, and seemed ready for anything. They advanced slowly, crouched, leaving her even less room for escape. They wrinkled their muzzles and ground their long, powerful teeth, growling and whining with excitement. For a moment Jole thought it was all over. She knew that their attack would be fatal. In the situation in which she found herself, it would not be easy to find a way out.

She thought about the reason she was up here, alone and vulnerable, and told herself that it could not end in such a brutal, stupid way. One of the wolves came even closer, as if to test her reflexes, to challenge her, a beginning to the dance of death. It was a ritual gesture, and it roused the other wolves, who picked up speed. They were now some twenty paces from her. Jole tried to swallow, but her mouth was dry. She could not let go, she must at least try to reach the rifle, even though she knew that if she ran towards the weapon the wolves would pounce. She clenched her fists and toes to bring the blood back to her limbs, which had grown rigid with fear. Behind her, Samson neighed loudly and started moving about and bucking. Jole felt ready to take the risk. Slowly, she took a step back. The wolves came even closer. She looked at them one by one, shifting her head from right to left, studying their movements to work out which of them would be the first to attack. Another step back. Then two more. The wolves, greedy and increasingly excited, crouched low, ever lower. Another howl from the same animal, who was older and mangier than the others. Jole turned quickly to check the exact position of the rifle. Seeing it, she turned again towards her predators.

Scenes from her childhood flashed through her mind. There was a strong scent of Swiss pine in her nostrils. The wolves had drawn very close. It was all or nothing now: her only hope of saving her life was to get to St Peter before those ferocious beasts leapt on her.

To gather her strength, she decided to count mentally to three, but when she got to two, one of the wolves on her left began to approach her threateningly.

It all happened in a flash. Jole broke into a run, but after three paces she stumbled and fell face down. Looking up and seeing that the rifle was now just a few centimetres from her, she reached out her right arm to seize it but was unable to do so. She reached out some more, stretching her fingers, but in vain. Out of the corner of her eye she saw the wolf getting ready to leap. With sudden force, she summoned all her strength of will and her desire to live and managed to lift herself just enough to move forward and grab the rifle. She wheeled round with all the energy and adrenaline she had and fired in the air. The shot echoed, as loud and cavernous as a powerful monster freed of its chains, and within a few moments all the wolves had drawn back a few paces in fright. Jole got laboriously to her feet and moved the rifle from right to left, aiming at her predators. Although they seemed as docile as dogs, they showed no signs of running away.

Breathing heavily, the fear still coursing through her veins like a river that has burst its banks, she took a deep breath and screamed threateningly at them:

"Go away!"

She took a piece of wood and threw it, hitting one of the animals. At this point the pack sensed that they were in trouble, and in no particular order they all began to withdraw to the woods below. Jole screamed again and fired another shot in the air, making it clear to them once and for all who was in charge.

The echo of the shot spread, bouncing off the faces of the mountains. The wolves, finally defeated, left in search of easier prey.

Jole stood where she was without moving. She had done it. God alone knew what saint had helped her after she had fallen to the ground and looked death in the face.

She heaved a sigh of relief. Her blood started to flow once more, so strongly that she felt the veins in her neck and temples bursting.

I don't think they'll be back. But the sooner I light a fire, the better. That's the only way I can be safe.

5

S TILL UPSET AND SHAKING from the terror she had felt, she lit a fire, thanks to the stones she had remembered to bring with her when she left Nevada. The first stars had already appeared in the sky, and beyond the southern profile of Mount Grappa a milky fog forecast the rising of the moon.

With the help of a few very damp branches, thick, heavy smoke rose from the fire. That, more than anything else, would keep the wolves at a distance.

Gradually Jole recovered. Using a little shovel, she started to dig a number of equidistant holes, forming a circle. When she had finished she stuck in them the longest, most resistant branches and tied the ends together. In the meantime, the fire had risen higher and begun to give off heat and light. She felt better.

Once she had tied the ends of the branches as tightly as she could, she laid over them all the blankets and cloths she had with her, and finally tied rope around the whole structure, quickly bringing her work to an end.

She fell to her knees in front of the fire, dead tired, and watched as the tongues of flame rose and slowly devoured the firewood.

She took out a tin saucepan and went and filled it from the spring. She drank several times, then turned back to the fire and stared, her eyes lost somewhere beyond the flames, beyond this place, these mountains and perhaps even beyond her life.

When you're alone, she told herself, *you must never trust anything and never take anything for granted. You must have a thousand eyes. Always!*

Her stomach contorted, but not from hunger. In the last few days she had eaten almost nothing, and yet she had no appetite. She knew, however, that she would have to eat, or sooner or later she would collapse. She took the red hen from the sack into which she had put it, twisted its neck with two abrupt, decisive movements, plucked it carefully, removed the innards as best she could, skewered it with a sturdy fir branch and moved it close to the fire. She turned it round and round endlessly, waiting for it to roast properly.

The stars were multiplying, trying to give the best of themselves before the radiance of the moon swept them away with its sovereign light.

Apart from the smell of meat on the fire, all around were the strong, persistent odours of the woods and the night – resin, mushrooms, pines – as well as sounds, ever more distinct and more disturbing: the distant howling of those beasts that had tried to attack her, the closer cries of the badger and the marten, and then the menacing calls of the barn owl, the scops owl and the pygmy owl. All at once she heard clearly the dark, mysterious, prophetic call of the eagle owl, and that evening, in that place and in that situation, it struck her as a truly sinister sound. It grew ever nearer and more disturbing, until she heard it coming from the handful of larches clinging to the crag right behind her.

She listened carefully. It seemed to her a timeless, eternal call, reminiscent of ancient eras. She had the impression that one day, when the world had disappeared, that call would remain as the last and only sound in the universe.

When her dinner was ready, Jole waited for the hen to cool down a little and cut it into pieces, ate part of it and put the rest in the jute sack, saving it for her next few meals.

She revived the fire with more wood and went inside the tent. She lay down on the ground and through the opening watched as the stars stepped aside for the arrival of the moon. Soon, though, she was assailed by thoughts of her parents. She closed her eyes tightly, but the harder she tried to think of something else, the more she saw again the same macabre scene she had encountered the previous evening. In a few moments she was overwhelmed with the awareness that never again would she be able to see them, embrace them, look them in the eyes, never again would she hear their voices. Terrified, she got up, went outside and threw herself down on the cold, damp ground. She was shaken with tremors, nausea, a sense of inner freezing and suffocation which paralysed her for a few seconds.

Then the worst moment finally passed and she got back on her feet. Her heart was a terrain of conflicting emotions: fear and courage, surrender and a desire for revenge, anxiety and relief.

Papà, she thought, *when I was eighteen, everyone assumed you were dead, but I didn't. In my heart there was always a little light, the slender hope that it wasn't so, the dream that I would see you again… But this time you really have left me. And so have you, Mamma. You've both crossed the only true border…*

While she was thinking these things, whispering the words to herself, the moon, instead of rising and dominating the sky, was dominated by it. From the west, layers of high clouds had quickly moved in. Soon, they covered the vault of heaven like an opaque veil over a mirror.

I'll think of you always. Be close to me every day.

The thought of her dead parents was for Jole an unconscious attempt to bring them back to life, to make sure their souls lodged themselves in her and guided her.

She walked over to a larch, the tallest of those around. She touched it delicately with her chilled hands, then embraced it, placing her cheek on its rough, strong, brown and red bark.

Only in this way did she feel better. It was like touching her parents, hearing them again, embracing them; as if they were inside that majestic tree, in its precious, living sap, but invisible to the eyes.

She recalled an old Cimbrian legend, according to which the larch is a magic tree, from the top of which, and down through the trunk, there descended the strength of the sun and the moon in the form of gold and silver eagles.

She sniffed the tree. It smelt of resin, and that smell soothed her soul.

She touched the dandelion pendant, felt a new inner calm and heard that voice gently but firmly summoning her back to a sense of loyalty.

Gradually the temperature fell, not only because the night was pressing down, but also because of a current of air spreading its icy tongue from the west.

She put two more logs on the fire, went back inside the tent and lay down, holding the rifle by her side.

"I swear on the grave of my mother and father that I'll find those bastards," she said out loud. "And you, God, if you're there, give me the strength I seek and then help me to leave."

The moon and the sky were now completely covered with clouds, and from the east a definite smell of snow was spreading, urged on by a wind that was sure of itself and its own voice. A voice Jole recognized immediately.

She stroked the rifle that up until two days earlier had been her father's. Then, as light and elegant as the flight of a redstart, her gaze wandered out of the tent and came to rest on the warm colour of the fire burning in the darkness of the night.

6

"NOW I'M GOING TO SHOW YOU how to make fire," her father told her when she was six. "You'll need it one of these days."

They had gone in search of mushrooms in the wood to the south of Godeluna, where Augusto always found lots of porcini and chanterelles, which Agnese would clean, cut into rings and chunks and leave to dry, to be eaten a little at a time during the following winter and spring.

In just under two hours they had already gathered more than two baskets and so her Papà decided it would be a good idea to stop and drink a little elderberry syrup and eat some forest fruits.

Jole was very happy whenever she went into the woods with her father, because with him by her side there was always something to learn, and often it meant having real adventures. Each time he would teach her new things: how to make tools, how to find unknown animals, how to recognize the secrets of plants and mushrooms, how to climb trees in search of wild honey.

That day he had decided he would teach her how to light a fire.

It was why he had chosen to stop in a sunny meadow far from the trees.

On the ground he laid an old piece of birch bark and some blades of dry grass he had just picked.

"Now comes the good part!" he exclaimed, bending down.

Little Jole, with her sly, curious gaze and her long blonde hair, sat down beside him with trepidation, as if her father were about to perform a genuine piece of magic.

"Watch closely," he said, taking two stones and a knife from his pockets. He showed her the stones one at a time. "This is flint, and this other is quartzite. If it doesn't work with one, it'll work with the other." He smiled.

He took the flint, positioned it between his thumb and index finger and then stuck the birch bark and the dry grass between his thumb and the flint. Then he started to hit the flint with the steel blade of the knife until sparks began to fly.

Jole had watched him in amazement. She could not believe that sparks could be created by those simple movements.

"You have to keep going," Augusto told her, carrying on undaunted, "until you get the right spark."

He worked at it for a few more seconds, always at the same rhythm and with the same intensity, until at last a good spark sprang up. Immediately, Augusto put the grass down on the ground, put more sun-dried blades on the flame, followed by a few small branches, then finally by bigger ones, until the fire took shape.

Jole clapped her hands and laughed with joy. "Bravo, Papà!"

"But now you have to keep it alive and make it bigger," he said with his index finger raised to the sky, as if this were a lesson.

She listened to him attentively, all the while gathering thicker and thicker brushwood and branches to feed the flames.

"It takes a lot of patience and care, as with all precious things," he said. "Above all you have to show respect, but you also have to be able to control it. Fire is important but at any moment it can become terrible."

"Are you talking only about fire?" Jole asked.

"Fire gives warmth and light, but it can also destroy."

"Just like people, right, Papà?"

Her father took her in his arms. "Fire is like a child, my girl. It's not enough to give birth to it. You then have to take care of it, otherwise it may vanish for ever or turn nasty."

7

B Y THE TIME JOLE OPENED her eyes it was already morning.
She woke with a tranquil mind, happy to hear, before
anything else, the singing of dozens of birds coming from the
woods: thrushes, robins, blackcaps, chaffinches. She listened to
them, following their interwoven melodies as if they were a song
of praise to the morning, a hymn to the sky. She thought about
Antonia, and how different her sister's prayers were to hers.

She considered what to do. The tent she had so hurriedly
built with makeshift materials had protected her from the
wind, which had whistled for hours on end, but not from the
cold. Even though she had fallen asleep under all the cloths
and blankets she had brought with her, her hands and feet
were frozen. She realized that she would have to move to get
her blood circulating again.

As she got up, she heard a continuous, insistent drumming
on a tree. Before long, she recognized the unmistakable call of
the woodpecker. She stretched, opened and closed her numb
hands several times, then put her head outside the tent to try
to spot the bird. The incessant clickety-clack of its beak made
it easy to locate, and indeed it only took her a few seconds. It
was clinging to the trunk of a beech, some ten metres up, a
glossy black, with the upper part of its head red and its beak
ivory-coloured. Jole looked at it and smiled with amusement.

She loved the black woodpecker. It was undoubtedly one of her favourite creatures. What she did not like at all, though, was the sky and the promise the clouds held.

For some time the days had been growing shorter, and in the dawn light she realized how yellow the grass of the meadows had already turned.

Jole went to Samson and stroked him, still scrutinizing the sky.

"We're going now, old friend," she said.

She drank some water, ate some black bread and speck, dismantled the tent and loaded everything on Samson. She wrapped herself tightly in her jacket, tied the red kerchief around her neck and put on the hat. Before mounting her horse, she saw a beautiful male chamois come out of the clearing and clamber quickly up through the trees.

She stood there for a few moments hoping to see it again, but it did not reappear.

Just like life, she thought. *One moment it's here, the next moment it's gone…*

She saw a little snowflake fall from the sky, immediately followed by another, and then another. Her face clouded over.

She was starting to worry: if the weather got worse, her mission would be much more complicated.

I hope my little brother has recovered by now, she thought. *But I know he's in good hands.*

She made the sign of the cross and set off again, up the slope of the huge massif.

8

THEY STOPPED FOR A MOMENT by a little spring. Water gushed up from the thin layer of snow that had accumulated in just a few minutes, glistened in the opaque morning light and meandered into a rivulet.

"They say there's even a waterfall round here somewhere," Ruggero said, panting.

Climbing on foot had worn him out. His face, already disfigured by the burn, had turned so purple as to make him seem more monstrous than ever.

Strim, who was even more exhausted than his accomplice, said irritably, "But why do we have to go all this way?"

"Don't ask questions!" Ruggero insisted, without stopping. "You just have to trust me!"

They were walking in fog, and the snow, even though fine and dry, was falling more determinedly now.

"I'm fed up with climbing!" Strim cried angrily.

Ruggero stopped and looked at him in silence, then lied to placate him. "It's not far to Cimanegra now. It's two or three hundred metres further up, after the forest of larches and Swiss pines you see beginning up there. I already told you, the house belongs to an uncle of mine who's gone to America. We'll be safe there for a while."

"Couldn't we have holed up in the caves near your mother's house, where we hid the ingots?"

"Do you really think the carabinieri aren't already looking for the people who killed those two old peasants? The daughter's bound to have informed them. They've probably found a whole lot of tracks in the mud by now. Do I really have to explain it all to you?"

Strim seemed to think this over for a moment.

Ruggero omitted to tell him that when they had got back down to the valley after the killings, he had realized he had lost the grey kerchief he always wore around his neck. It had probably fallen off during the struggle with Augusto.

He went on, trying to be even more convincing:

"And who would they look for first, eh? Have you forgotten you spent time in prison, you old pig? Think about it: we stay up there for a few days, nice and quiet, and then we go back down."

Strim grunted, but in the end agreed to the plan.

They resumed walking. An icy wind set the snow swirling, forcing them to squint.

Two hours earlier they had left the horses further down, sure that, if it continued to snow, the legs of their scrawny nags would barely be able to make it through.

Strim stopped again, caught his breath, took his mouth organ from a pocket of the sheepskin he was wearing and started to play.

Ruggero wheeled round. "Do you think now's the time?"

Strim, who was also carrying the knapsack with the provisions and the bottles of grappa, continued to play regardless.

"Put that damn thing away!" the thin man cried, shielding his face from the increasingly strong, snow-laden wind.

Strim gave him a sidelong glance, calmly put his mouth organ back in his pocket and resumed walking, bending forward a little to cushion the force of the wind.

9

AFTER AN HOUR'S JOURNEY, Jole reached a second plain, higher than the first, and from there rode though a big spruce forest, over which the broad fronds of the trees provided a dense covering.

Although the snowfall was dense and persistent, the undergrowth had remained almost dry and the flakes were having difficulty settling even on the treetops, because it was *brüskalan*: light, dry, powdery, clean-smelling snow.

All at once Jole heard a noise behind her. First a resounding creak, then a very loud crack of immense force that produced a tearing, throbbing sound in the air. She wheeled round and immediately realized that she was in grave danger. The violent, ear-splitting noise was in fact the clamour caused by a huge spruce that had snapped beneath the weight of the years and was about to crash right on top of her. Jole saw the tree move slowly, but once the roots came away from the ground the trunk gathered speed, bearing down on her like a peregrine falcon swooping on a dove.

"Run, Samson! Go!"

Jole grabbed the horse's reins and started moving forward and to the side to get out of the area of impact. But just when they thought they were safe, the top of the tree struck Jole a glancing blow, throwing her to the ground.

She landed on her side, but did not seem to have seriously hurt herself. Now, though, she had to free herself from the branches that were keeping her from moving. She clutched hard at some rough, twisted roots emerging from the ground like exposed nerves and tried several times to pull herself out. She focused her strength and her thoughts, counted to ten and tried again. One attempt, two attempts, three attempts. She managed to gain a few centimetres, but not enough to free herself of the grip of the great conifer.

"Samson!" she cried desperately. "Come here, come closer."

The horse loomed over her. With a great effort Jole arched her back and grasped with one hand at the leather bag tied to Samson's left flank. After several attempts that led nowhere, she finally managed to grab hold of the top of the rope and slip it off the bag. She made a slipknot at one end and tied it to one of Samson's hooves, then clutched the rope with both hands and cried:

"Come on, friend, now pull. Ya! Ya!"

Samson moved, as resolute and strong as ever, and in a few moments, Jole was freed from the heavy grip of the branches, albeit with some difficulty. She got to her feet and caught her breath.

She heaved a sigh of relief: the blow she had received would not limit her search, would not cut short her mission.

She bent over Samson and untied the slipknot, put the rope back in its place, again donned her crumpled hat, which had ended up under the branches, and kissed the horse's muzzle.

"Bravo, my friend."

She made the sign of the cross and looked around, alert to any suspicious noise, sniffed the air like a fox that senses the presence of strangers and got back on her horse.

10

S HE MANAGED TO GET her bearings easily thanks to the
moss clinging to the trunks of the north-facing trees. After
crossing the whole forest, she came to a village consisting of
some ten or so houses of highly unusual construction, although
Jole had heard of them: large houses with *sfojarol* roofs, that is,
roofs made out of beech branches and leaves. They were the
typical stone dwellings of the Feltrino area, built on higher
ground to catch the last rays of the day's sun, with terraces
used for drying various crops.

Encouraged, convinced she had reached Cimanegra, Jole
continued to ride slowly and, out of caution, took the rifle
from the side holster. The landscape was white, and as she
proceeded solemnly, the snow fell on her hat and her face.
There was not a soul about, but she assumed that was due
to the bad weather. Metre after metre, though, she realized
that this village had actually been abandoned. High weeds
peeked through the snow on the main street and everywhere,
between one house and the next, lay work implements that
had rusted. Swift as a stone marten's, her eyes darted from
side to side. She took care always to cover her back. The
houses, all locked with chains and padlocks and half-covered
with climbing plants and wild brambles, seemed to have been
empty for a while. All around was a deep silence and the

very few sounds that came from the surrounding forest were muffled by the snow, which was still falling, blurring every outline.

Jole dismounted, gripping her rifle tightly, ready for anything, and began walking around these strange buildings. When the wind rose she took shelter under a *mazól*, a protrusion of the roof that protected the front door and facilitated the ventilation of the attic.

She was in a genuine ghost village, one of the many in the Prealps and Alps that had been abandoned in the last few years and would soon, inevitably, be overrun by the surrounding forest.

Then she looked up at the roofs, those strange coverings of leaves, branches and plants, and saw the chimneys, dozens of them, none giving off smoke. Except one. Jole's frozen hands tightened on her St Peter and she advanced cautiously towards that house in the middle of the village from whose chimney grey smoke rose. Moving a few metres, she peered into the stable, and there, sure enough, she recognized the horses belonging to the two criminals. She felt a shudder go through her, because the sight of the animals recalled to her the fetid smell of those two vermin.

Furtively, hugging the walls, she moved closer to the house. Then, when she was only a few metres from her objective, she aimed the rifle at the front door and got ready to flush out her two enemies. Just then, she spotted beside the house a short, hunchbacked old man with firewood in his arms. When he saw her he dropped his load in fright and cried, "Don't hurt us, we don't have anything, we're poor people!"

Jole looked at him in astonishment, thinking it might be a trap. "Who's in the house?"

The man gave a small, respectful bow. "My wife and I are just poor old people. I beg you—"

"I'm looking for two men. One is short with a deformed face and the other is as big and fat as a bear."

At these words the man's wife appeared. Her face tense with fear, she said in a supplicatory tone:

"Yes, we saw them, they passed this way two hours ago, when it was starting to snow, and left in a hurry. They left their horses in our stable here. You can look for yourself!"

The man glared at her. "What are you saying? Are you mad?" he cried angrily. "Do you want them to kill us when they get back?"

"Why should I trust you?" Jole said. "How do I know they're not hiding in your house?"

"Believe me!" the woman replied, almost kneeling to convince her. "Why would I have told you about the horses? It's just that we're scared."

"Is this true?" Jole asked the old man.

He seemed terrified, reluctant to speak.

"Tell her!" the woman said to him. "What's the worst that can happen to us now? What could be worse than this solitude?"

The old man plucked up his courage. "It's the truth!" he said. "For heaven's sake, I beg you, don't hurt us…" He was whimpering like a child now.

Although Jole had the feeling these people were genuine, she did not lower her guard. "Let me inside," she said, "I want to see!"

"Come!" the old woman said.

Jole went into the house and searched all three dark, mouldy-smelling little rooms, including the spinning room. Once reassured, she lowered the barrel of her rifle, sat down by the *larín*, the kitchen hearth, and asked the man if hay could be given to her exhausted horse. The old man was pleased to oblige. He went out to fetch Samson and feed him, then came back inside.

The house was very old and very poor, made of spruce beams, with a central architrave that supported the whole roof. Next to the hearth was a wooden crucifix adorned with interwoven branches of silver fir. The floor was of packed earth and every corner of the room smelt of burnt wood, smoke and cast iron. Jole thought of her own home, and the gentle eyes of that solitary old couple reminded her of her own parents.

A timeless feeling emerged both from the gestures of those two old people and from the objects present in the house. Through the little window with the deep recess, snow could be seen falling from the sky. The flakes had grown bigger and heavier, a sign that the temperature was rising.

The old woman gave Jole warm goat's milk to drink and offered her some Montasio. Then, while her husband continued looking down at the floor with the fixed stare of someone prey to huge anxieties, she told her how those two ugly mugs had turned up.

"They scared us, the way they bossed us about," she said in a thin voice. "I thought they were very bad men. They said they'd be back for the horses in a few days because they had to continue their journey and with this snow the horses would be a problem. They threatened us with knives, said they'd burn the house down if we didn't do what they wanted. The fat man kept playing a mouth organ. They left in a hurry."

"Which way did they go?"

"I don't know. When they left, my husband and I barricaded ourselves inside the house for fear they'd kill us."

Jole did not tell them why she was looking for the two men, only that they were both criminals.

"May God protect us!" the woman cried, made nervous by all these visitors in a single day.

They were all silent for a few minutes. Jole closed her eyes, savouring the milk and enjoying the warmth spreading through her almost frozen hands and feet. More than once she breathed deeply. She remembered Sergio. She hoped they were looking after him in the convent and that he was recovering.

"It's clear you're a good person," the old woman said.

"Why?"

"You can tell from the eyes."

"There aren't good and bad people," Jole said resolutely. "There's only goodness and badness."

The old woman seemed to think this over and then said, "Holy words… These days school teaches many things."

"I've never had a day's schooling in my life. My school is the mountains."

The two old people looked at her incredulously.

"Do you mind telling us where you're from?" the man asked.

Jole looked at him kindly. "I'm from Nevada, on the other side of the great valley."

"So near and yet so far…" he said, staring into the fire. "Nobody ever comes this way, you know how it is… There were lots of people here once, but they've all gone away, in dribs and drabs. I don't know where it'll all end, it's a disaster! Even the priest has left."

"Did they all go to America?"

"So they said. Especially to Brazil. And to Argentina. But some also to the United States and even to Mexico."

"And how much does the journey cost?"

The woman spoke up again at this point.

"The 'promisers' who came here kept saying that the price was negotiable. They told everyone they'd be able to pay with what they had in their houses, so the other people in the village loaded everything on their backs and went down… including our children and grandchildren."

"Do you miss them a lot?"

The woman looked at the fire in the *larín* and slowly shifted her gaze to the window, as if trying to hide the two little tears running down her face and into her deep wrinkles.

The old man resumed. "I'm sure they're better off there than here. Everywhere is better than here these days. They say America is a beautiful place. Open fields, fertile land, lots of work, food for everyone, wealth. The 'promisers' say it's the land of plenty, where you can eat and drink your fill."

He stood up laboriously, struggling with his aching bones, and went and threw a beech log onto the insatiable white-hot hearth.

His wife continued to look outside the window, with deep sadness in her eyes. "Some today, some tomorrow," she said, "and in the end only my husband and I will be here until we die, or for as long as God wants. We make do with what little the vegetable garden, the hens and the goats give us. But oh, how we miss the old days, when we were fine and there were so many of us up here… Where could two old people like us possibly go? It's a long journey, and I've heard that lots of people die crossing the sea."

Jole listened to them with compassion. Whole villages and towns were disappearing because of poverty, the fault of a government and a king who let their own citizens, their own subjects die of hunger. She felt a mixture of anger and pity, as she usually did when confronted with the injustices she saw every day, at every moment, everywhere.

That damned, filthy, eternal, diabolical border between the poor and the powerful, between the humble and those who abused their authority.

"My wife and I will remain here to the end, where can we go now?" the old man said in a tone of deep resignation. "This is the place where we were born and have always lived, and here we'll end our days."

"That's right," said the old woman, her eyes lit by glimmers from the cast-iron hearth. "This will be our last homeland."

Jole wondered what a homeland was, if words like that ever meant anything, or if, rather, they were concepts designed to divide men, like barbed wire.

She remembered the eagles and the dandelions she had seen on either side of the border.

All identical despite the stupid flags of men.

"The last homeland?" she asked after a few seconds.

"That's right," the woman replied.

Jole stood up and embraced her as if she were her mother.

We poor people are all citizens of the last homeland, she thought, allowing herself to be welcomed into the woman's thin, stiff arms.

But she must not let herself be distracted from her mission. She realized she had procrastinated for too long. She came straight to the point.

"If this is Cimanegra," she said, "then where can those two men have gone?"

"No, this is Almeda," the old woman said.

Jole almost choked on her last sip of milk. "Almeda? So that's why... And where's Cimanegra?"

"Higher up. On your horse it'll take you just over two hours. After the hermitages and the witches' waterfall. But there's nobody left in Cimanegra either. Do you have to go there?"

"It's where those two are probably hiding."

"If you like," the old man said, "for the first part of the way you can follow the mule track. Your horse is a lot stronger and sturdier than the other two. And besides, this weather won't last. It's already warming up. The snow will stop tonight, and tomorrow the sun will melt everything. And it's only November."

"Let's hope so," Jole said, smiling. "Samson isn't afraid of anything anyway. In his life he's seen it all."

She got to her feet and headed for the door, putting her hat back on as she did so, feeling refreshed by the warmth of the *larín*, the hot milk and mature cheese.

"Please, I beg you," the old man said, walking her to the door, "if you see those two again don't tell them we told you these things. They really scared me. I wouldn't want them to do us any harm. You know, my wife talks too much..."

"Don't worry," Jole said, looking at him with gentle, sincere eyes, "I won't say anything and they won't be doing any more talking either, believe me!"

"May God bless you."

Jole collected Samson and mounted him. A few heavy snowflakes were still obstinately falling.

It's turning to bachtalasneea, quail snow, she thought. *It'll melt soon. It's better so.*

As the old man had predicted, the clouds were breaking up, opening here and there to let the late-morning light through.

Jole was pleased. One problem had been lifted from her shoulders. Without snow, climbing would be easier. She felt new blood flowing in her veins, warmer and thicker, giving her a sense of invulnerability.

She thanked the two old people and bade them farewell.

"Ya!" she cried, urging Samson on, and the steam of her breath emerged from her mouth like smoke from a chimney.

She started up the whitened mule track and continued on her way with the tenacity and determination of a hungry marten on the trail of two squirrels.

Ruggero and Strim had two or three hours' head start, but they were on foot now, whereas she was on horseback.

11

T HE TWO MEN HAD ENTERED the larch forest beyond
which they were sure Cimanegra was situated.

The snow had stopped falling, but the climb was still laborious and Strim kept complaining.

He stopped again, took his knapsack from his back, extracted the bottle of grappa and took a swig.

"This damned snow was all we needed!" he cried, more irritable than ever.

"We're nearly there, you can't keep stopping every ten metres!" retorted Ruggero, who was a few paces further up. "Just think, once we've arrived, you'll be able to rest, drink and play that stupid thing you stick in your mouth for as long as you like."

Strim glared at him. Then he drank some more from the bottle and said:

"You'd better pray we are nearly there, my friend, or I'll be really angry. When I think we could have stayed down there and hidden in those damned caves!"

"It's one thing hiding the ingots for a few days, another thing being down there ourselves. And besides, I'd like to see you sleeping in a cave. You were pretty pissed off last night sleeping in that hut."

"I can sleep anywhere! Anything would be better than a trek like this, damn it!" He fixed his companion with a surly, hostile stare. "And look, the snow isn't even high anymore! It's actually stopped snowing. We could have come up here with the horses. It would have been a lot less bother!"

"We're not turning back!" Ruggero said firmly.

"Of course we're not, but with the horses we'd have been there by now. You and your idea that they might break their hooves!"

"The horses will be perfectly fine in that old couple's stable. They're in the warmth and they're eating. Nobody comes up as far as Almeda, not even the crows. And anyway," he added with a sneer, "when we go back for them we won't leave any witnesses…"

Strim looked at him knowingly. He found the idea of killing the old couple, the only people left alone in that mountain village, highly exciting.

They continued their ascent and Ruggero, in an attempt to keep his accomplice in a good mood, decided to remind him how much they had enjoyed doing away with those two peasants in Nevada.

"When you stuck the pitchfork in his belly, I split my sides!" Strim exclaimed.

Ruggero laughed. "Right to the end, they wouldn't admit they had them, even though we knew perfectly well where they kept them hidden. He was asking for it, and so was his wife… Though you didn't have to stab her in the back."

Strim drank some more. "So much fuss over a woman…"

They advanced a little further, panting and stopping ever more frequently to catch their breath. They were almost at the end of their tether.

"Tell me," Strim suddenly blurted out, "what did you think when the girl, the daughter, showed up at your mother's? After we'd been stalking them for days, there she was, right in front of us."

"I was afraid one of them might have seen us, but I soon realized she was there for my mother. It did us a favour anyway. Having only the two old folks to deal with was a walkover."

"True! It must have been one of your mother's miracles."

"She can't perform miracles any more than the devil can."

Strim laughed with delight, then grunted. "When I saw her in front of me, so close, I felt like having her there and then, that little minx."

They both laughed heartily.

And before continuing on their way, they decided to drink more grappa.

12

EVER MORE DETERMINED to track down the two men, and reinvigorated by her halt in Almeda, Jole set off along the mule track on the faithful Samson, ready to begin yet another ascent.

Thanks to her horse's strong temperament and natural inclination to hard labour, she proceeded at a fair pace, even though the snow on the ground came up to well beyond his hooves.

Jole decided to keep the rifle with her at all times, since she might come across the two men at any moment. As Samson advanced, she looked around cautiously, ever on the alert. She was riding through a wood of black pines, spruces and Alpine beeches, whose trunks, grey and dappled, reminded her of the skin on the face of that woman who had given her hospitality, that poor old woman, so gentle, so caring.

And so brave, Jole thought. *Because it takes courage to leave, but it also takes courage to stay on your own…*

They were surrounded by a cocoon-like silence. The clouds were moving like waves in the sky, opening, rising higher and turning from snowy white to increasing grey. Every now and again, over and above the soft, rhythmical sound of the snow crunching beneath her horse's hooves, the song of the Alpine accentor and the call of the white partridge rang out.

Jole thought again about how she and the old woman had embraced, and the strength that gesture had conveyed to her. And from there her mind wandered to Sebastiano, the Cimbrian *pechér* she had met in the woods near Sasso and with whom she had fallen in love.

How I miss those embraces…

As she advanced through the cold, the air blowing on her face, the exertion of the journey, the memory of that first kiss flooded over her. She almost felt as if she were reliving the experience. A tremor ran through her body and she quivered with the emotion of it, a warm, sweet emotion just like the one she had felt back then, when he had looked deep into her eyes and put an arm behind her waist and, gently but firmly, drawn her closer to him. Then, for the first time, their lips had slowly come together and the initial light touch had turned to an intoxicating rapture. She recalled the taste of his mouth, delicate and insinuating, and his brown skin and his hair, which smelt of pine resin. And she was still stirred by the memory of how he had kissed her on the neck, how his hands had rested on her breasts and touched them, how he had kissed their tips, how their bodies had swayed together like two blades of grass in the meadows, one beside the other, moved by the same breeze.

On that horse in the middle of the snow that covered the back of Mount Grappa, hunting for two criminals who had slaughtered her parents, it seemed to her that she could feel those sensations again, just the way she had then.

The games life plays with us. God knows where he is now…

For a while, she could not get him out of her mind, although she had to remain focused on her journey and the surrounding

154

landscape. She thought again about her few encounters with him in that wood, when, hidden from the eyes of the world, they had fallen in love and their bodies had played together like two squirrels pursuing each other up and down the branches of the conifers.

All at once she thought she heard the call of a cuckoo. She pricked up her ears.

Let's hear in how many years' time I'll get married! she thought, remembering the old folk belief.

She heard the call again:

Cuckoo-cuckoo.

"In two years' time!" she exclaimed, laughing. "Heaven only knows where I'll be in two years' time…"

She stroked Samson's neck, clutched the dandelion pendant and came back to the present, because while dreams do not kill us, we cannot live on them either.

13

A T THE SAME TIME, Sergio was in a small room in the
infirmary of the convent of San Girolamo.

The nuns, who alternated prayer and meditation with work
in the kitchen gardens, had put him in a small ashwood bed
and were taking turns in keeping an eye on his condition. As
soon as the boy had arrived within these walls, the apothecary
nun had begun an investigation into the possible causes of his
illness and the best treatment to pursue.

Convinced that she had grasped the nature of his illness,
she had decided to make him fast for a day and a night and
apply leeches to the points of the body where the main arteries
ran. Once this treatment was over and he had been cleansed
of his infected blood, Sergio had been given two spoonfuls of
rhododendron honey and syrup of propolis every half hour and
infusions of nettles, olive leaves and artichoke roots every hour.

After a few hours of treatment, the delirium had ceased
and the fever passed, and thanks to these remedies Sergio had
woken from the torpor that had held him in thrall.

As early as the following day he had felt rather better, at
least well enough to keep his eyes open and start to take a few
spoonfuls of soup.

The little room in which he lay was completely bare apart
from a small oak crucifix hanging on a wobbly nail above the

door, on which the face of Christ was disfigured and worn due to repeated falls to the floor.

Often left alone now, Sergio did not know how to pass the time. He would lie for hours listening to the sound of the bells and the sacred chants coming from the church, and looking at the crucifix constantly, waiting for it to fall so that he could then call someone to come and pick it up and hang it back on the wall.

Or at least he would have liked to, if only he could.

Because every time the crucifix fell to the floor, he was not able to call anyone.

Not because he had changed his mind.

Quite simply, the words did not come.

He wanted to speak, wanted to say something, to give voice to what was going through his head.

And yet he could not. His mouth would stay closed, clamped shut.

His will and his head could not reconcile.

And he would remain mute. Speechless.

He would look at the disfigured Christ on the floor, nailed to the cross, face down.

And, incapable of speaking, he would keep silent.

14

A T MIDDAY THE CLOUDS thinned out, evaporating and scattering in the light, and the rays of the sun came to rest on the ground and the snowy expanse. The temperature decreased and the snow began to freeze on the surface.

Jole and Samson continued without a pause. She was encouraged by the change in the weather, which made it easier for her to find her bearings and see what was happening around her, even in the distance, without having to trust her other four senses.

After an hour and a half, as predicted, she came to an abandoned hermitage beside a small watercourse that descended parallel to a larger stream some fifty metres further north.

Circling the outside, she saw that it was dedicated to St Helena. She said a prayer to the saint, about whom her mother had often spoken to her, and decided to have something to eat, since the cold was consuming a lot of energy. She took two pieces of hen from the jute sack and finished them, one bite after another. Then she drank from the stream alongside Samson and filled her canteen.

She resumed her journey with much exertion, but surrounded by a landscape of incredible beauty. Everything around her was white. The blue sky and the vistas stretching to the Austrian border in the north, the Asiago Plateau in the west and the Friulan Dolomites in the east took her breath away.

On the expanse of snow that descended southwards in a gentle slope, Jole saw a pair of white partridges flying about, and on the opposite side a hare sped across a small pass.

She took a deep breath. She felt part of this world, this nature, the mountains and their spirit, knowing perfectly well that without these landscapes she would not have been herself, she would not have had the same feelings, would not have been the same person. She would have become a different woman, a different Jole. She felt nostalgic for it all. Like the shadow of a distant knowledge, kept hidden until then, but destined inevitably to reappear. She looked around, trying to seize all of that wonderful, sublime expanse, and make it her own with a breath, to store it as if by magic inside herself, in the treasure chest of her own spirit, her own heart. For ever.

She remembered when, travelling to the border at the age of sixteen, she had become aware of her father as an ancestral being, a spirit as wild and free as a lone wolf. And right now, this was exactly how Jole felt. Perhaps it was only the awe of the moment. Or perhaps she really had inherited from Augusto a feral, primordial nature. It was likely that the blood of the De Boers was connected with the shamans of the Norse legends Jole had heard so often as a little girl from her Cimbrian grandfather, who claimed Scandinavian descent.

Twenty minutes later, continuing her climb, she came to a pass and, a few metres further on, a signpost, a wooden arrow fixed to a post stuck in the ground. She went closer to read it, but the sign was covered in snow. With her right hand she wiped away the snow.

She could barely read, but she understood that it showed the way to Cimanegra.

She sniffed, spat on the ground and continued in the direction indicated until, a quarter of an hour later, she came to the ruins of a Benedictine hermitage and then to a small but enchanting waterfall, whose thunderous sound seemed like the deep song of the whole surrounding landscape. After ten more minutes, she reached a cave of dolomite, grey limestone and marl set in a face of the northern slope.

She saw someone in the distance, a man by a fire. Jole tightened her grip on her rifle and approached with great caution. She was tired, but that did not mean she could relax her vigilance.

When he saw her, he raised an arm in greeting. He had two donkeys with him.

She looked at him: he was not one of the two men she was looking for. He was young, with a light blond moustache and the beginnings of a beard. Not far from where he was sitting were what must have been his work tools: a series of pickaxes, clubs, hammers, mallets and chisels of all sizes, as well as containers filled with stones.

Many were those who climbed up from the Belluno Valley to tickle the entrails of the mountains and the Grappa massif in the hope of extracting minerals and precious stones to be sold at a good price, once they had been cleaned and polished.

There beside him, indeed, were various items of equipment for filtering the raw materials that had been scraped from the cave walls: a pestle machine with a moving trough, a grid through which to pass the crumbled stones and small fragments of mineral, buckets of water, portable stoves for the roasting of the materials, as well as other tools, among them brushes of all sizes to clean the minerals, bottles of vinegar to wash them, saws to cut them, and sandpaper and glass wool to smooth and polish the gemstones.

"Good day to you," he said by way of greeting, with all the joy of someone who has not seen a living soul for weeks.

"And to you," she replied, still on her horse and keeping her distance.

"Are you hunting?" he asked.

He had the tired, pale face of someone who has worked hard, perhaps with meagre results. He was very young.

"Yes, I'm hunting," Jole said, glancing at the barrel of her St Peter and resting it on her shoulder.

"Pity about the snow," he said.

"On the contrary. It slows the deer down."

He laughed. "I'm looking for minerals," he said without her having asked. "Malachite and amethyst. It's hard to find decent quantities, but they're easy to see. I'm from Feltre, what about you?"

She looked at him curiously. "I'm not from Feltre," she said.

"Are you interested in some stones? They're beautiful, you know, really shiny. There's a green and a purple like you've never seen. I'll give you a good price."

"No, I don't want anything," she replied curtly, touching her pendant. "Do you know the way to Cimanegra?"

"It's up there, but further east, less than an hour anyway. If you want to get there quicker, you can take that shortcut there." And he indicated a point close to a forest of larches.

Jole looked in that direction and thanked him. Then she took a piece of hen from the jute sack and ate it.

15

"HOW MUCH FURTHER?" Strim asked, exhausted. It was early afternoon.

They were in the middle of the larch forest, and even though the sun had come out and there was not too much snow along the path, both men were tired of walking. In addition, Strim was ever more irritated by his accomplice's decision to trek all the way up here.

"We're nearly there," Ruggero said.

With two big strides, Strim caught up with him and gave him a suspicious sideways look. "What about the kerchief?" he asked quietly, catching his breath.

"What kerchief?" Ruggero replied in a sharp, nervous voice.

"The one you always wear round your neck. Where is it?"

The thin man passed a hand over his neck, embarrassed. "I left it at home. It was choking me."

"But I've seen you wearing it for years!"

"That's why it was choking me," Ruggero said, cutting him short and resuming his trudge between the high red-brown trunks of the larches. "Let's save our breath. We're nearly there."

Strim threw him another mistrustful look. "I need another drink," he said, again taking out the bottle of grappa.

"Look, I'm going ahead on my own!"

"Go ahead," Strim said. "As long as I've got the booze!" And after taking a swig, he put his hand back in his knapsack and took out his mouth organ.

Ruggero, not only exhausted but hysterical by now, pounced on his accomplice like a wild cat, tore the instrument from his hands and threw it as far as he could.

Strim stood there, stunned. He watched as his mouth organ flew between the branches of the trees, fell some way below them and sank into the snow with a soft thud.

16

JOLE SET OFF in the direction of that larch forest, but then brought Samson to a halt so she could look around and think. Should she trust the advice of that young man with the blond moustache?

Mindful of the terrible experience that had marked her two years earlier, it was her opinion that it is never good to trust appearances, not even when you think you are dealing with decent people.

All the same, the wild instinct that had lately developed in her had also taught her to scent particular dangers and become aware of their sinister presence. And she did not have the feeling that this young man searching for precious minerals was untrustworthy or mendacious.

She turned to look at him once again. He was waving at her. She responded by raising an arm. She looked up to where stretches of snow-covered meadows alternated with patches of spruce, making it hard to see the top of the mountain, then back down at the spacious and more gently sloping forest of larches. She thought this over for a moment and decided to heed the young man's advice. Just then, a red squirrel with very dark fur descended, head down, from one of the first trees in her path.

There'll soon be only animals left in this land, she said to herself.

This she was thinking as she proceeded towards Cimanegra, while Samson sank his hooves in the snow, never slackening his pace.

"And what is this homeland?" Jole asked herself, her voice soft in the muffled silence of that landscape. She ventured between the first larches. "Homeland and border are two sides of the same coin. My true compatriots are those who live through the same misfortunes as me, in the same period."

Then a sixth sense made her alert again. She heard the muffled clicking sound of a grouse coming from below, behind a stretch of blueberry and rhododendron. She brought Samson to a halt and inspected the landscape of trees around her. There was nothing untoward. On the ground she saw the tracks of a hare and nothing else. A little further on, though, something attracted her attention. She dismounted, holding the rifle, and went to have a closer look. At first she did not believe it, but then she realized that it was true: they were the tracks of the two men. There could be no doubt about it. They crossed her own trail at right angles and aimed straight for the top of the slope. She crouched down and looked up: a stretch of larches and those four tracks moving into it as far as the eye could see, stopping every ten or fifteen paces.

Jole's heart rose to her throat. Her hands, cold until a moment earlier, began to sweat and grow warm. Her mouth went dry and she felt a quiver of incredible excitement. A sensation of euphoria and adrenaline. A desire for retribution mixed with fear and courage and a hint of madness. She recalled her father's voice when he urged her to do great things, to overcome certain difficulties, to overcome her own fears. Then she seemed to hear her mother's gentle voice, to feel the strength of her serenity, the warmth of her loyalty.

Bastards! She clenched her teeth. *I've found you! I knew I'd find you!*

She told herself that snowfall had been a gift from God, since everything leaves a trace on the snow. She wanted to cry out. Not only had she found them, but all she had to do now was follow those tracks, like the wolf that follows the scent of the lamb. She took a deep breath. She realized that nothing had yet been done, and she would have to keep up her concentration and remain vigilant, because those two might be only a short distance away. She gripped her St Peter resolutely and stood up, repeating out loud some words her mother had said to her.

"Hope doesn't mean being sure that things will go well, but being convinced that they have a meaning, however they end up."

With a sardonic smile, she got back on her horse and began to follow the tracks of the two murderers. They were close. She could feel it.

17

RUGGERO DA RONCH and Richard Strim had both been born thirty-one years earlier, in 1867, a few months after the Veneto was annexed to the Kingdom of Italy.

The former never knew his father. He was born in a village near Vas, not far from Belluno, but he and his mother immediately moved to Sedico, then to Belluno, and finally returned to Vas, where the two of them settled into a house that had belonged to a great-aunt. To make ends meet, Ruggero, still a young boy, started robbing and swindling people in the markets and fairs of the neighbouring villages, while his mother began passing herself off as a healer, mainly practising clandestine abortions by administering bicarbonate and concoctions of poisonous herbs. At the age of sixteen he left home and started living off his wits, resorted to crime, and soon ended up in jail for armed robbery, assault and, on a few occasions, even murder. One way or another he had never stayed there long. Either bribing the guards or escaping, he had managed to regain his freedom and had gone back to his previous life, but not without some unforeseen events, like when a woman caught him robbing her house and threw a pan of boiling oil in his face.

Strim was originally from the Biois Valley. He had been born in Somor, a little village between Falcade and the San

Pellegrino pass. He had lost his parents in a fire when he was seven and had been adopted by a cousin of his uncle's, who had brought him up like a father, until, when still a young boy, Strim ran away from home and started stealing, drinking and living the criminal life. He was ruthless. He never backed down. In many Dolomite and Prealpine valleys south of the border, it was said that on his raids he had not even spared the lives of children. He, too, had ended up in prison and it was behind bars, in Campese, just a year earlier, that he had met Ruggero. The two men got along well from the start and, once they had escaped from prison, started roaming about, committing terrible crimes, and sharing the spoils of their misdeeds. They operated mainly in the area around Marostica and to the south of Bassano, sometimes extending their activities as far as the Upper Padua area.

The idea of tailing Augusto De Boer had come to them a few weeks earlier, one morning early in the autumn of 1898, when they had found themselves in the workshop of a man in Cassola who made copper pots, and had seen him exchanging two ingots of copper for money and provisions.

This had aroused their suspicions: they had wondered where this man, a poor peasant, could have acquired those ingots.

Putting pressure on the man, even threatening to kill him, they got him to confess everything, including his dealings with a tobacco grower from the mountains. They decided to tail Augusto.

Augusto himself had not noticed anything, and several

times led the two criminals to his house. Watching day after day, they figured everything out, and located all the places where the De Boers' little treasure had been hidden.

18

AFTER A FEW MINUTES, Jole dismounted and lay down on her side, still as a doe in a clearing and on the alert for any strange stirring in the air, any suspicious noise.

She adjusted her big hat, rubbed her frozen hands and wriggled her toes in her boots to keep warm.

The sky was now clear of clouds and the sun quite high.

The snow on the ground was starting to melt and the white mantle on the ground glistened like snow in May.

Blocks of compacted snow fell from the branches of the larches, exposing their autumnal colours.

As long as they don't disappear... she thought, looking at the two men's tracks, then set off again, her rifle ever ready to fire.

She felt nervous but strong, and knew that whatever happened, the very fact of having come this far and having discovered and flushed out those two bastards was an achievement in itself, even if not yet a success.

For her path, her journey, her adventure to really be concluded, she would have to find them and do what she had to do.

Jole had always been convinced that animals, just like human beings, felt emotions, and at that moment, advancing slowly between the larches after those four big, heavy male prints, she felt like a golden eagle following the tracks of a marmot from above.

It was as if she were flying, describing a circle in the sky, awaiting the right moment to close her wings and dive down on her prey in the middle of the meadow.

She stopped again and smiled.

She bent and tilted her head slightly to the right.

She put an open hand behind her left ear.

She heard something coming from above, a few dozen metres further up.

She listened.

They were male voices. Two of them.

Her heart began to pound and she held on to Samson's neck.

19

AT THAT VERY MOMENT, Antonia was kneeling in the convent church for the recital of the rosary, united in contemplation with the other fifty-two sisters.

A little earlier, she had been to see Sergio in the infirmary. Entering his little room, she had picked the wooden crucifix up from the floor, hung it back on the wall and tried in vain to get her brother to speak.

Then, sitting on the bed, she had prayed for him, and left thanking God for saving him. She was pleased with the treatment the apothecary nun had prescribed.

She had retired for a few minutes to her cell, where she had knelt on a very hard yew prie-dieu and prayed for the souls of her mother and father.

Requiem aeternam,
dona eis, Domine
et lux perpetua luceat eis
Requiescant in pace
Amen.

She had looked out through the little window that gave onto the smaller cloister, in which stood three kinds of evergreens, as a constant reminder that faith, hope and charity never yield their leaves to the earth either.

They were two small olive trees, a large, luxuriant magnolia and seven cypresses as tall and upright as two hands in prayer pointing to heaven.

It was only then that she realized the weather had changed over the previous few hours.

What had, on Mount Grappa, fallen prematurely in the form of snow, in Bassano had manifested itself as a persistent cold drizzle bathing the roofs and streets of the city.

Antonia had pulled her black shawl around her shoulders and observed the sky, feeling as if that silent, humble water falling to the ground were the tears of Mamma and Papà.

Then she had remembered her sister, and a shiver of fear went through her.

She had no idea where Jole was or what she was doing.

And that scared her.

All this had happened to her before going to the church for the recital of the rosary.

When the mother superior began the *Salve Regina*, which preceded the other prayers, Antonia thought once more of her sister.

> *Salve, Regina, Mater misericordiae,*
> *vita, dulcedo et spes nostra, salve.*
> *Ad te clamamus, exules filii Evae*
> *ad te suspiramus, gementes et flentes*

in hac lacrymarum valle.
Eia ergo, Advocata nostra, illos tuos
misericordes oculos ad nos converte.
Et Iesum, benedictum fructum ventris tui
nobis, post hoc exilium, ostende
O clemens, o pia, o dulcis Virgo Maria.

"I beg you, Holy Virgin, protect Jole."

20

JOLE TIED SAMSON to the trunk of a tree and climbed back on foot, careful to remain hidden by the vegetation and holding St Peter as if it were the most precious thing she had.

The voices of the two men, one shrill and piercing, the other cavernous and explosive, grew ever louder, as if they were quarrelling.

At last she saw them.

It was the second time in her life that she had seen them, but the first in which she knew them as the killers of her family.

The fact that they were so close was unsettling.

They struck her as more vile than ever. They were panting, their faces ruddy. The one with the disfigured face was speaking as if he were on the defensive. The fat man looked ready to jump on him.

"Go and pick up my mouth organ!" he cried in a peremptory tone that seemed to brook no reply.

The thin man was silent for a moment. He did not move, as if these words had not even reached him.

"It's nothing to do with me," he said eventually, his voice slurred because of his dangling lip.

Jole crouched down, trying to work out what was happening.

"I told you to go down and get the mouth organ! I'm not going to repeat myself, you son of a whore!"

The other man smiled mockingly. "Come on, let's get out of here," he said.

At this, the fat man let out a grunt and leapt on him like an enraged bear.

Jole watched in astonishment as the two men fought in the heavy snow, punching, rolling over like two boars, insulting each other and cursing.

After a while the thin man managed to free himself of the other man's grip and got back on his feet. His mouth was mangled, his face swollen from the blows.

"I'll show you... You asked for it..." he said, spitting blood. He took out a big knife and waved it at his accomplice. "You asked for it, you bastard!" he repeated. "My mother may not be a saint, but she's no whore either!"

It all happened in a flash.

The thin man threw himself on his accomplice and tried to stab him with a downward blow.

Despite his size, though, the fat man managed to dodge the blow and roll away. When he got up again, he was holding a pistol. He opened fire and hit the thin man in the right thigh. The thin man fell to the ground, screaming in pain.

Faced with this scene, Jole was petrified. The fat man did not waste a moment, but immediately fled down the slope, heedless of the fact that he had dropped his knapsack in the excitement. A little way down he picked something up from the snow and vanished amid the larches, abandoning his wounded companion for ever.

The thin man was screaming in desperation, cursing his tormentor and trying in vain to get up again. He put both his hands on his leg and swore. Then he laboriously removed his jacket, took off his shirt and tied it tightly over the wound, between the knee and the groin. He put the jacket back on and crawled like a snake as far as the nearest tree. Clinging to a branch, he managed to get back on his feet.

"I'll kill you, you bastard!" he screamed down into the valley.

It was at that moment that Jole snapped out of her inertia.

She slipped out from the hazelnut tree behind which she had been hiding. The man found himself looking into the barrel of a rifle.

Although Jole's hands were shaking, her eyes blazed with fury, like those of a mother bear defending her cubs.

"Here you are at last, son of a whore!"

He stood there motionless, his mouth wide open, bleeding. He raised his hands in surrender, incredulous. He looked at Jole as if she were an apparition, a mirage, an irrational nightmare. He fell to his knees.

"You…" he muttered, blood still gushing from his leg. "You…"

"Yes, me!"

"It… It was Strim! It was that bastard! He was the one who—"

"Killed my mother and father?"

"Yes, it was him!"

"My family was everything to me," she said, eyes watering.

"It was him, I swear!"

A malicious, cynical smile appeared on Jole's face. "You're a bastard! You killed my mother and father!" She spat at him, and the spittle landed a few centimetres from him. "Bastard!" she repeated.

"If you let me go, I swear I'll… I'll give it all back!"

Jole thought this over. "All right. If you tell me where the ingots are, I won't kill you."

"I knew you were a bright girl, I knew it!" he exclaimed, despite the terrible pain in his leg.

Jole looked at the two knapsacks left on the ground during the fight. "Take out the ingots!"

He looked at her imploringly. "They aren't there, but I swear I'll tell you where they are if…"

With her rifle still trained on him, she rummaged in both knapsacks, but did not find anything that interested her.

"Where are they?" she cried, harder than stone.

He ground his teeth and screamed in desperation from the pain. "In the Oliero caves."

"Why should I trust you?"

"I'll take you there. We'll go together!"

"So why did you come all the way up here?"

"We had a shelter, an abandoned hut, a bit further up. We were sure the carabinieri… I never thought you…"

Jole stared at him as if looking at something obscene. In her eyes there was hate, but above all, a demand for justice. She would not kill him. She would leave him here to die.

"The Oliero caves? Is that the truth?" she asked, threatening him.

"Yes!"

"That's where the ingots arc?"

"It was Strim: he did everything. It was his idea to kill those two. He forced me to help him."

"So he's on his way to the caves?"

"Of course he is, the son of a…" Trying to get up, he screamed from the pain in his leg, which was bleeding profusely. "Now that I've told you, you won't kill me, right? You promised!"

Jole looked around. They were completely isolated from the world. More than ever, she felt part of the forest, sister to all its animals and plants, as fierce and beautiful as its laws.

"No, I won't kill you," she said, lowering the rifle and aiming it at the man's good leg.

"What… what are you doing?" he stammered.

Jole pressed the trigger and a lead bullet reduced his foot and left calf to pulp. Although the snow muffled all noise, she nevertheless heard the echo of the shot, and the smell of gunpowder spread through the surrounding air. It was the smoke of justice, and Jole opened her nostrils wide to breathe it in. The man, now deprived of both his legs, fell forward, face in the snow, tortured by the pain but now incapable, once and for all, of getting back up. He tilted his head to one side and his wet face turned pale.

Jole raised the barrel of the rifle and rested it on her shoulder, satisfied, as if she had finished a good job.

"I'm not going to kill you, you son of a whore. The wolves can do that."

Ruggero was moaning and weeping, blood gushing from his legs.

In the distance wolves could be heard howling.

"There they are. They're already on their way," Jole said, touching the dandelion pendant.

Then she turned her back on him and walked down into the forest to collect Samson.

I'll catch up with him in a few minutes.

She untied her faithful horse, mounted him and before leaving looked again at the big, long tracks scattered along the slope.

The howling of the wolves came closer.

21

"Ya!" she cried, setting off in pursuit of Strim.

On the one hand she was convinced she would catch up with him quickly, but on the other she knew that in the snow she couldn't force Samson to go too fast. And she had to be careful: Strim had a gun with him.

From a distance, she turned once more to look at the monster in his last moments of life.

She did not feel any pity, hoping rather that the wolves would arrive soon, sink their teeth into his flesh and pack him off to hell.

While Samson descended between the larches, puffing through his nostrils, and Jole thought again about her mother and father, the sun was starting to set and its rays to grow colder. The sky was clear and deep, as if it wished to welcome and cleanse all of Jole's thoughts, all her breaths.

She noticed that there was less space now between the fugitive's footprints, a sign that he had slowed down: he was tired, but he had no idea that he was being followed.

This was always my great advantage, and still is, she thought. *Neither of the two knew that I was coming after them…*

In any case she had to catch up with him as soon as possible. She could not afford to be overtaken by sunset: that would mean losing all trace of him and putting off the pursuit.

She decided to make Samson go faster.

"Ya!" she cried.

Jole emerged quickly from the wood and reached a stretch of *haapar*, the melting snow still visible in patches on the meadows. She urged Samson on ever more insistently. But after galloping along for a while, the horse struck a hoof on a small protruding rock and stumbled.

22

W HEN SHE CAME TO, her head was spinning and she ached all over.

Jole could not tell if she was awake or dreaming. She was lying on the ground on a red and green cloth, wrapped in a blanket. Around her everything was dark and silent. Only the crackle of a fire could be heard in the distance. She tried squinting, but in vain. Everything was wrapped in darkness.

Little by little, she began to distinguish the shapes around her. She was inside what remained of a mountain cabin, a precarious, rotting old *tabià*, the kind of barn-like construction where shepherds in the pastures spend the night during the fine season.

She looked through the window and saw a tongue of fire. And the stars in the sky. She was hot. It seemed to her that the temperature had risen.

She tried to lift her upper body and succeeded. She leant on her elbows, raised her hand to her head and realized it had been bandaged with a long white cloth.

She made out the form of her horse beside her. He was eating hay and did not seem to have any injuries.

"Samson!" she exclaimed, smiling. "You're all right!"

At that moment, a shadowy figure approached her.

Jole groped around for the rifle, but did not find it.

When the shadow at last took shape, Jole stared open-mouthed.

"Are you feeling better?" the girl in the fur hat asked.

It really was a dream, Jole thought: what she was living through could not be possible.

She could not believe that there in front of her was the same shepherdess she had met two years earlier on her way back home.

"Is it really you?" she said, holding her head. "Maddalena?"

"Yes, it's me," the girl replied, with a very sweet smile that brought out her big dark eyes. Her two long-haired spotted sheepdogs appeared behind her.

It seemed as if no time had passed for her, even though the life of a shepherdess was hard and full of toil. Jole looked at her in admiration. The girl really was beautiful.

Even her clothes were the same as before. She was still wearing that strange fur hat with the fox tail that covered most of her dark hair.

Jole tried to get to her feet, but the shepherdess motioned to her to remain seated, and held out a steaming cup.

"Drink! It's made from herbs I gathered in the pastures during the summer. It'll do you good."

Jole took the cup from her hands and sipped the aromatic infusion with pleasure.

"Running away again, are you?" Maddalena said.

"This time I'm not running away, I'm following!"

"How life changes, eh?"

23

T HEY CHATTED A LITTLE and Maddalena said that by chance she had been on the other side of the clearing when she had seen her galloping down and falling to the ground. She had immediately gone to her rescue and brought her to this nearby cabin.

It had not seemed to her a bad fall, although when she had arrived on the scene with her dogs she had found Jole unconscious.

"And where are your sheep?" Jole asked.

"With their owner until next summer, in a mountain cottage above Arten."

"So what are you doing here?"

"As it happens, and luckily for you, I'm on a pilgrimage from the hermitage of Santa Lucia to the hermitage of San Bovo, and then to San Giorgio di Solagna... A few days' walk in the company of Pelmo and Marmolada, my sheepdogs."

Within a short time, Jole felt better: the pains faded and the dizziness ceased almost completely.

"That herb tea of yours is miraculous!" she cried.

"It's the mountains that are miraculous. You just have to know what they offer," she said, and began delicately to remove the bandage from Jole's head.

Her face was stained from earth, fire, air and water, and yet it was delicate and mellow.

"Look!" Jole said, showing her the pendant she wore about her neck.

Maddalena gazed at it in astonishment.

"It's the dandelion you gave me, remember?"

Maddalena laughed, revealing slightly crooked but very white teeth.

"Of course I remember!" she cried happily. "Have you managed to stay strong?"

Jole's eyes were watery and on hearing these words there passed in front of her in a flash all she had been through in the last few days, in all its brutal, cruel truth.

She felt herself collapse suddenly, as if her mountains were crashing down on her heart.

She began to weep, and the shepherdess hugged her tight.

Jole felt an incredible heat go through her, something that not only warmed her, but regenerated the fibres of her body and fortified her spirit. Two years earlier, too, this girl had transmitted the very same sensations to her and she did not understand how it was possible.

She looked her in the eyes, sniffed and wiped her face with the back of her hand.

"It's just like we were sisters…" she said softly, incredulously.

Maddalena smiled at her. "Yes. It's just like we were sisters."

24

W HAT WITH THE FAINTING and the accumulated tiredness of the last few days, Jole had slept for almost ten
hours on end and now could not wait to set off again. She had
lost a lot of time because of the fall and was afraid that Strim
might escape her, together with the ingots.

She was aching all over, of course, but not as much as
before. She had a mission to accomplish, and there was no
obstacle that could stop her from continuing.

"More haste, less speed," Maddalena said in an almost
mystical tone. "And anyway you still have to rest. You can
wait for the first light of dawn. Night strips every man and
lays him down to sleep." She looked at the sky outside. "It's
going to be a beautiful day and even the little snow remaining
up here will soon melt."

In the clearing outside the *tabià* the presence of a large
number of deer could be glimpsed and above all heard.

"There must be at least forty," Maddalena said, pleased.

They finished the old hen that Jole had with her, and then
the shepherdess opened one of her bags and took out some
stale bread, some Morlacco and a canteen full of water.

"What happened to you?" Maddalena asked. "You said
you're following someone. But you haven't said who and
why."

Jole sighed, and in a few laboured words told her the whole story.

They were both silent for a while, without even looking each other in the eyes. Then Maddalena said:

"Just before witnessing your fall, I saw a man running down. It must have been him."

"It is him!"

Maddalena put more wood on the fire and began looking at the stars. "Revenge doesn't pay," she said in a low voice.

"I don't want revenge, I want justice!" Jole said almost angrily, raising her voice. "And in this case justice means those ingots. Everything my father and mother had. Those ingots are my past and my future, and I want them back!"

Maddalena listened to her in silence, calmly. "Maybe you're right. Who knows?" she sighed. "And then?"

"And then what?"

"What will you do once you've obtained justice?"

Jole fell silent, put her head on her knees and began to weep, her long, loose hair flowing down over her legs. "And then…" she stammered. "What is there left for me to do? I'll do what everyone is doing now…"

Maddalena looked at her sadly. "You'll leave?"

"Yes. I don't have any choice. What else could I do here?" she sobbed. "Don't you think it's possible to leave your own land?"

The young shepherdess looked down at her old, worn, mud-caked boots. "If crossing the border means travelling without knowing where to go and therefore how to grow," she said, "having a homeland means recognizing ourselves, knowing who we are and what we will be."

Maddalena was saying things Jole did not entirely understand. She stopped crying and raised her head to look at her.

"For human beings," Maddalena went on, "having a homeland is what having soil is for trees. It's the place in which we can grow, put down roots, feel strong. But not all kinds of soil are good for all trees. And when storm winds blow strong, then whole forests are uprooted."

"I don't think I quite understand."

Maddalena looked her in the eyes and whispered, "If you feel it, do it! If you feel you have to leave, Jole, then leave!"

She stood up, walked out of the *tabià*, faithfully followed by her two dogs, and threw another spruce log on the fire, which began to crackle loudly.

Jole lay down again under the blankets and closed her eyes, listening to the crackling of the fire and the singing of the nightingales, which seemed to be competing as never before, ready to give the best of themselves before dawn.

Together with their singing Jole became aware of the rustle of the leaves, and then the remote voice of a stream, the distant cry of a scops owl, and finally the blowing of the wind. A cool wind, newly risen, and yet the same wind that accompanied her everywhere and spoke to her, whispering the truth of things and showing itself exclusively in the beauty of its movements. The same wind that came every time from the north, from the border where they had known, respected and loved one another, and which went with her on every important journey, never abandoning her.

And finally the silence. A deep, rare silence. Because sometimes even in the forest there can be silence, even at night.

Lord, she thought, *give me a heart capable of listening to this wind.*

She reopened eyes shiny with tears and looked at the starry sky through a big gap between the beams of the roof.

She fantasized being with Samson, galloping through wide woods of silver firs.

She imagined every tree turning into a star and found herself, as if by magic, riding in the firmament. A vast firmament in which to wander for ever, until you felt useless and lost as a birch leaf beneath the January snow.

Immediately after that, though, she was permeated with another sensation: an amazing sense of freedom. The infinite joy of having no more obligations, no more chains, no more ties. Nothing at all. Her future showed itself to her, as wonderful as that starry sky. It was at that moment that she knew it for certain: after dealing with Strim she would leave.

25

W HEN SHE WOKE, she was alone.

The fire was out and from its ashes emerged a small column of white smoke that rose thin and straight towards the sky.

Maddalena had gone, having left her a cup of herb tea and some rusks on a log placed just outside the *tabià*.

The sun was low, still hidden behind the ridge of the massif, but the day looked like being clearer and warmer than the previous ones, especially after the squally weather of the day before.

The air smelt of mountain pine and honeydew and was clear enough to give glimpses of the plateau to the west, the Lagorai chain and even the Pala range to the north.

Jole stretched. She still ached a little, but basically she was fine now and even her head felt light, her thought process rapid.

She thought about Maddalena, her ever mysterious and fascinating figure, and was upset that she had gone like that, without giving her the chance of another embrace.

With that magical, enchanting and at the same time elusive aura of hers, Maddalena seemed like some kind of *anguana* or water sprite, a sylph from a Dolomite stream. Jole drank the tea and ate the rusks, then went to fetch Samson, and as she did so she remembered the words the shepherdess had spoken the night before.

She shooed the last horseflies of the season away from Samson's muzzle and stroked him.

She inspected his hooves, his abdomen and his ribs. He was fine.

"My faithful companion…" she whispered to him.

The horse let his muzzle and his muscular neck be stroked.

"If we have to part, you'll forgive me, won't you?"

She collected her things – provisions and rifle included – and arranged them on the horse.

Then she tied her hair, fastened the red kerchief around her neck, put on the big hat and set off, stronger and more determined than ever to settle accounts with Strim.

This is the day! she said to herself as she began the descent towards Almeda.

She was certain that the killer, convinced he was safe and sheltered from any danger, would not move from the Oliero caves for a while.

The most important day of my life coincides with the last day of his, she thought, the sense of predestination reinforcing her confidence in her own strength.

26

S HE DESCENDED THE WESTERN SLOPE through dense
woods of spruce and meadows on which the snow had
now melted, leaving the space to grouse and quail. She
entered a splendid beech wood and even there she could
see that, after the bad weather, the mountain animals had
roused themselves again and reappropriated the undergrowth
and its damp floor. Above her head she spotted a fierce
goshawk flying silently between the branches in pursuit
of fleeing squirrels. Then she saw a fox, a weasel, and a
greater spotted woodpecker hammering at a beech trunk in
search of insects, and heard the song of a pied flycatcher.
She stopped for a few minutes to drink some water and eat
a little Morlacco. She set off again immediately, thinking
anxiously of the elderly couple who had given her hospitality
on the way up.

She arrived in Almeda and was encouraged to see smoke
rising from their chimney, a sign that they were alive and well.
She rode past their house, slowed Samson, peered quickly
inside the stable and saw a single horse, which must have been
Ruggero's. She did not stop, not even for a moment. Instead,
she tightened her hands on the reins and urged Samson to
descend at great speed.

By the time the old man came out of the house to wave to her, she had already disappeared beyond the sinkhole on the outskirts of the abandoned village.

27

I N LESS THAN TWO HOURS she reached the first and second plateaus she had crossed on her outward journey. Once again she descended the steep, slippery slope covered with broad-leaved trees overlooking the deep canyon, and at last came out into the narrow Brenta Valley.

I'm sure Sergio is fine now, she thought.

She proceeded without feeling any strain, or any hunger or thirst – except a thirst to track down that bastard.

She reached Valstagna, crossed the Brenta and set off along the old road beyond the right bank of the river. Luckily, that slope of the mountain was already touched by the rays of the sun and was almost dry. She stopped for a while in a meadow above the road to let Samson graze.

It was well into November, and yet that morning it was definitely warmer compared with the previous days, so warm that Jole was forced to take off her heavy jacket and put it in one of the big leather bags hanging from Samson's flanks. She looked around and fixed her eyes on the face of the mountain from which she had just descended. Its crags were dark as night because of the snow and the rain, and the woods that clung to its slopes were now almost completely bare and as prickly as a porcupine.

High up, in the portion of sky standing out exactly halfway

between Mount Grappa and the plateau, a pair of eagles were circling. Their spiral flight was slow and confident: it was as if those two majestic, relentless birds lived beyond time, as if they were stronger than time itself, as if they flew unaware of, and indifferent to, the inexorable succession of the days and nights.

Jole felt moved as she gazed at them: among all the animals she loved, the eagle had a special evocative power over her, and whenever she saw one she was held in a kind of magic spell.

A magic spell that imbued her with gentleness and strength.

28

S HE QUICKLY RESUMED the trail going south. She reached the hamlet of Oliero and from there at last came to the caves, in the vicinity of which were forges, a couple of water-mills, a few sawmills and a paper mill.

Jole rode to the stream of the same name, barely a hundred metres long from its origin at the caves to where it flowed into the Brenta. She looked at its shallow water, as green and transparent as her eyes, and moved over to the sinkhole behind the paper mill. There, the entrance to the main cave could easily be seen, the waters of the stream gushing forth placidly.

It was impossible for the workers in the forges and the paper mill to see her where she was. She proceeded slowly on horseback, careful both to see and not be seen.

God, please let him be here! she thought, clenching her teeth.

Hidden amid the birches and wild lime trees that covered the little hill, she loaded the rifle and leant out to look from above at the cave entrance and the bed of the river, some ten or so metres below her.

She saw Strim's horse tied to an ash.

"Thank you, God!" she said softly.

A few metres from the horse, near the mouth of the cave, was a tiny raft formed from thin conifer trunks. It had been attached to a weeping willow, whose pendulous branches lapped the surface of the water.

Jole dismounted, swallowed, cracked her fingers and stretched her back.

"Wait for me here and be good. I'll be right back," she whispered to Samson, tying him to a lime tree.

Then she lowered her head and bent her back and began to descend the grassy hillock, clinging to the branches of the trees in order not to slip. The silence was pervaded by the constant, tranquil murmur of the stream. Strim's horse neighed when it saw Jole coming, but she stroked it and calmed it down. Cautiously, she made her way over to the little raft.

She untied it from the willow, got in, placed St Peter across it, seized the wooden pole and slowly pushed herself towards the cave entrance.

The stream was so deep and the current so calm that it only took a few thrusts to reach the dark, troubling mouth of the cave. Jole made the sign of the cross, gave another thrust and glided in.

The ceiling was so low that she had to bend her head. The inside of the cave was completely dark, and for a moment Jole cursed herself for not having procured a torch. Gradually, though, her eyes grew accustomed to the darkness and she was able to see again, helped by the dim sunlight coming in behind her. It was then that she spotted a second source of light: a glow some fifty metres ahead of her that cast monstrous, terrifying shadows over the walls and tunnels of the cave, shadows that seemed to Jole as if they were ready to leap on her and eat her up. She had to move as silently as possible. Very calmly, she put down the pole and in its place seized the rifle. She managed to put aside her fear and keep calm and clear-headed, and soon she realized that the glow must be being produced by a lantern or a torch: she had found Strim.

A shiver ran through her chest and down her back, but she mustered her strength, telling herself that destiny was on her side: that was something she had understood after the night spent with Maddalena. She put down the rifle, took hold of the pole again and with it pushed herself slowly forward with three more thrusts.

The cave was filled with stalactites and stalagmites of every shape and size, tall and protuberant, thin and bulging, some of them looming over her head like the huge, sharp, drooling teeth of some mythical monster. Down with the pole, up with the rifle.

The light of the sun behind her gradually dimmed until it disappeared completely, and from that moment on she could count only on the mysterious glow that just then seemed to move and change direction.

She grew worried and felt disorientated. She could not tell if it was the torch that had moved or if the stream had changed direction. The glow became ever weaker, as if whoever was holding the torch were about to hide inside a tunnel or behind a wall. It was only now that Jole realized how vitally important that light was for her. If she lost sight of it, she would be plunged into darkness and would have to try and find her way back in the pitch black.

Down with the rifle, up with the pole. Forward, three more thrusts. In total silence.

The light appeared again, although its flashing reflections on the surrounding walls were deceptive and misleading. She saw it in front of her, then on her right, closer now.

She came to a small landing place, with another raft identical to hers beside it. She pulled over and got out. She picked up the rifle and moved part of the raft onto dry ground to prevent it being carried away by the current.

From there a shiny, slippery path wound its way through a myriad of stalactites and stalagmites. That was the side the torchlight came from, somewhere beyond those chalky rocks, some of them sharp and pointed, some as soft and round as the snow on the roofs of houses after a blizzard. Her heart was pounding, and her legs started to shake. She had the terrible feeling that she was about to run out of breath. She who loved open, boundless spaces, meadows and forests and pastures, the wind blowing on her face and in her hair, felt suffocated in that cage of damp rock. Confined in the dark bowels of a mountain in a massif of the plateau, she doubted, just for a moment, that she would ever get out of there.

29

S HE SHOULDERED ST PETER and, taking care not to stumble or slide, she followed the torchlight like a moth. The glow came and went, disappearing and then reappearing in an unsettling way, as if whoever was holding that torch had become aware of the presence of an intruder and was moving to escape or to disorientate her. Jole kept going, clinging mentally to her past and to the extraordinary strength of spirit she had always demonstrated, despite all difficulties.

She advanced, turned right, then left, climbed and descended two flights of steps, careful not to hit her head on the protruding rocks.

From the first, she had had the feeling that she was in a maze, and now she was sure of it. She stopped, tried to reason, to listen carefully.

She heard small, repetitive noises that resembled the patter of boots and that seemed to follow the movements of the light.

After a while she heard a strange noise and the light went out.

Jole stopped where she was and in the total darkness listened to the sombre echo set in train by the fall of the torch.

When the noise stopped echoing between the walls of the cave, she heard only the pounding beat of her own heart.

Then the light returned.

Taking care not to make any noise, Jole moved forward a little, silently, slowly, weighing every move and every step, hoping with all her heart that her enemy had not become aware of her. She passed a wall of stalactites and suddenly there he was. It really was Strim, with his bear-like frame and his huge furry eyebrow.

With one hand he was eating something, and with the other holding up an oil lamp. His shadow was cast on the wall behind him, enormous and terrifying, and to his right were various things thrown haphazardly on a kind of pallet. It looked for all the world like the lair of some wild man of the woods: stinking blankets, bags, a knapsack.

The man seemed to have been taken by surprise and when he saw Jole and the barrel of her rifle, right there in front of him, he froze.

"I... I..." he tried to say.

"They were my mother and my father!"

"It was the other fellow! I didn't..."

Jole continued to point the rifle at him. "You'll have to suffer," she said. "Tell me where the ingots are!"

"There," he said, jutting his chin out in the direction of the knapsack on the pallet.

Jole went to the knapsack, opened it and saw the eight ingots she had been looking for. She closed it and put it on her back. "These things are mine!" she cried angrily. "And—"

Strim did not let her finish her sentence. In a fraction of a second, and in three very quick moves, he dropped the lamp, took out his gun and fired.

But in that fraction of a second Jole also fired, rooted to the spot and finding herself in darkness, pitch darkness. The deafening noises of the two shots echoed for a long time. Jole was not immediately sure if she had been hit or if she had managed to hit her enemy. But then she realized that she was still on her feet. Cautiously, she retreated, moving through the smoke from the shots.

She heard an object roll towards her and come to rest on the tip of her boot. It was the lamp. A moment later the sound of wheezing rose from the ground, somewhere ahead of her.

She gathered up the lamp. Luckily for her, the little flame had not gone out completely.

Another deep, lumpy wheeze rose from the floor.

Jole took shelter behind a chalky rock and raised the lamp high, expecting a shot, which did not come. Gradually she lifted her head above the rock and peered straight ahead.

"Damn!" she said between clenched teeth.

She came out from behind the rock and approached him with no fear now. The bullet had torn through his right fore-arm, and in falling back Strim had impaled himself on a pointed stalagmite. It stuck out from his abdomen like a huge bloodstained tooth.

It was a horrible sight, and Jole could only look at it for a moment or two. She turned away, retching.

Her head started spinning and she felt the veins in her neck throb, as if her heart had suddenly gone mad. Beads of icy sweat ran down her forehead, and her hands shook. She fell to her knees, exhausted, drained.

"Damn!" she said again, and heard the word echo around the cave.

After a few minutes she got back on her feet, lengthened the wick in the lamp to revive the light and slowly retraced her steps to the raft.

She got on it and a few minutes later, like a baby coming into the light, Jole, too, blinded by the sun flooding the Brenta Valley, came back out into the world, in a kind of rebirth.

She did not know what to say, or what to think. She had a feeling that justice had been done, but she also felt lost and confused. She had just reached the bank of the stream when a gust of wind blew off her hat. She gathered it and put it back on her head. She tied the raft to the willow, went back to Samson at the top of the hillock and set off, the ingots safe on her back.

PART THREE

1

S HE HEADED NORTH, knowing perfectly well where to go. The sun was high and strong and strangely warm for the time of year. From the hamlet of Oliero as far as Valstagna, she rode along the right bank of the Brenta, passing dozens of people descending on foot towards Bassano to emigrate.

Most sang old folk songs from their own valleys. Some laughed, excited perhaps by the change they were living through. Others wept, unhappy at leaving their lands. All were laden with cases and bags. The women wore long, dark dresses, their heads covered with big floral-patterned scarves, while the men wore hats of straw or fustian. Those men not chewing tobacco had cigarettes clamped between their lips.

Jole looked at them with new eyes, feeling in a strange way that they were waiting for her to join them.

She watched them with sadness and hope, and with the awareness that these good people were in desperate search of a new land, a land that would give them more joy and more bread.

She saw a child of perhaps five or six, and it struck her that joy without bread is like a valley without a mountain.

She proceeded slowly until she had passed Valstagna, since what she had to do she had already done, what needed to be accomplished had been accomplished. She felt worn out, in body and in spirit.

While Samson cropped a little yellowed grass, she spotted in the distance, on the other bank, two carabinieri on horseback. They were out on patrol. She watched them with a mocking smile, wondering what benefit those vain, colourful uniforms had brought the poor people of these mountains.

She rode through the Frenzela Valley along the main road and then veered off it onto another path. Engrossed in her thoughts and anxieties, she did not realize that she was advancing at some speed until she reached the meadows on higher ground.

She was pleased with what she had done, and yet she was troubled by a strange sensation. She kept asking herself how she felt and did not know how to answer her own question.

She was not sad or embittered, but nor did she feel contented or happy. She was sure she had done the right thing, and yet something was tearing her up inside.

She reached her destination. It was the church of San Francesco, between Foza and Stoccareddo, where she had often gone on pilgrimages with her mother and where Antonia had been in the habit of going alone before deciding to become a nun.

She dismounted, unsteadily, and went inside the church. She knelt in front of the altar and burst into tears like a little girl.

At that moment, she realized for the first time that she was alone.

She had decided the night before to visit that church and ask God for validation.

And now, her hands joined, that was what she did.

2

S HE ATE WHAT LITTLE she had left – some *sopressa* and some old Asiago – then went to a well not far from the church, from which both she and her horse drank. Then she washed her face and arms while the warm sun bathed her.

Finally she lay down on the ground in the meadow with its autumn colours. She looked into the heavens and wondered if the souls of the dead really did end up there, as the priests said. In her opinion, it was not true at all: she preferred to think that they were reborn as trees in the forest or flowers in the pastures or crystalline streams that descended continually from the highest peaks of the mountains. Or else as clouds, like those that passed over her head. Or as breaths of wind…

She got back on her feet and mounted her horse again.

"Ya!" she cried. "Let's go home for the last time."

3

WHEN SHE REACHED Nevada she had the feeling she had been away for weeks, perhaps months.

She stopped at the top of the hill overlooking the house where she was born, and for a moment her heart beat more loudly. In the blue sky a number of small white clouds had formed, looking like huge goose feathers resting on a crystal surface.

She let her gaze sweep the landscape, the setting in which she had lived her entire life. There was a lump in her throat from the emotion and a shudder ran through her body and lodged in her chest. It seemed to her that in all the world there could not be a place more heartbreakingly beautiful than this. Wherever she went, no other landscape would be able to replace it in her heart.

She sat there on her horse, spellbound by the meadows below, and seemed to see herself as a little girl.

She watched herself as she learnt to walk in front of the house and her father and her mother, very young and with eyes filled with strain and a sense of the future, laughed and joked with her when she fell on her backside. Then her father took take her in his arms, lifted her and kissed her, and so did her mother.

Then she looked some more and saw herself when she was a little older, running about and playing everywhere and with whatever she could find, never stopping for a moment, because she had always liked running wildly.

She saw her father putting her on his back and, surrounded by a flock of tits, carrying her to the *masiere* to show her the tobacco plants. Then her small, shy sister Antonia also appeared in the meadow, and finally Sergio. She saw all of them laughing and joking, sitting on the bench outside the house on a summer evening as the sun set. And then she saw the house and the meadows covered with a thick, copious layer of snow. It was all white and soft. A warm light glowed in the little kitchen window and thick, resin-scented smoke rose from the chimney.

Jole was moved.

She came back to herself and looked at what was really before her eyes on that November day in 1898.

The empty, uninhabited house. Not far away, next to the larch wood, her parents' grave.

The first thing she did was ride down to it.

When she came to the cross, she dismounted and sat down next to the mound of earth in silence, while two white wagtails passed close to her with their sinuous flight and elegant tails.

She took a deep breath and for the first time, even though she felt all the weight of the last few days collapse on her, she felt lighter, almost as though the inner upheaval she had been through were dissolving like fog in the sun. She felt a serenity and an inner peace make its way into her breathing, instilling in her a pleasant limpidity, what her mother would probably have called "contentment".

"I'm here," she said softly, looking at the grave and gently touching the dandelion pendant. "I'm back!"

She was aware of a quiver coming from the sky, from the woods, from the mountains beyond the *masiere*.

From the branches above, the song of a mistle thrush and the shyer song of a great grey shrike rang out.

The afternoon air began to grow cooler. She put on her jacket and remained there beside them, without saying anything else, her thoughts wandering like a thousand brooklets flowing down a slope and waiting to merge into a single stream.

The hours passed, the beautiful puffy clouds dissolved and the sky turned orange, then pink, turquoise and finally blue. The first evening stars appeared and still Jole sat there.

She finally got to her feet when the Great Bear and the Milky Way appeared above her.

The Milky Way must really be a great road, she thought, and perhaps her mother and father were travelling along it right now to some unknown destination. Then she told herself that wherever her parents were now, they would see her anyway and would smile at her, approving everything she had done. She was certain that from that day on they would always guide her at every moment, every second of her life, wherever she went.

She rode to the house and led Samson into the shed. At last, for that night at least, he would have a roof over his head and plenty of hay.

She removed from his back the burden of his harness and all the sacks and pouches he had been carrying. Finally she slipped the rifle from the long leather holster in which it was resting, carried it up to the loft and put it back in its hiding place.

"This time it really is for ever," she said, putting in the last nail and sniffing her hands, which smelt of old iron.

That, too, was a kind of burial.

She climbed down from the loft and went back to her beloved and faithful Haflinger.

"You're one of a kind," she said to him, stroking and kissing him on the cheek. "This is going to be hard for me."

Then she went into the house, lit the stove and a few candles and moved through the rooms, gathering memories, tears, smells, voices and sounds. Everything, every single shade of memory, every detail of the past, came rushing into her heart, arousing mixed emotions, tears and laughter.

She put a large pan filled with water from the Brenta to boil on the cast-iron stove in order to make a plate of soup with leftover cereal and a few vegetables that were still in the pantry, preserved from the autumn cold.

In the meantime she gathered a few clothes, some objects that were dear to her and everything she had left there the previous time, when she had left in haste and fury to take her brother to the convent and embark on her adventure.

She stuck everything in a large jute sack.

She found the biggest pot and took it into the bathroom. She poured water into a large stone basin and at last was able to wash herself with hot water and a little soap made with ashes from the stove and marmot fat.

She undressed and immediately got goose pimples because of the cold. But as soon as she touched the water, her body relaxed and all her muscles loosened. The bath, makeshift as it was, restored to her body and her long hair all their enchanting beauty, but above all gave back purity to her spirit. Cleansing and rinsing her body seemed to her to purify and renew her soul, too, bringing her back to an inner peace she had once had, but had not felt throbbing in her limbs for too long now. She felt beautiful, but above all proud to be a woman.

She dried herself as best she could and went back to the kitchen, exhausted and with her hair still wet. She stretched out on a bench in the warm atmosphere of the *stube*, where before long her hair dried. She finished cooking the soup and ate it straight from the pan with a ladle.

The smell of these rooms and these walls, she thought, would be by her side at every moment of her life. She would take it away and have it with her always.

Tomorrow would be an important day, a very important day. For now, though, she just had to think about sleep and rest as nature intended.

She took a candle and was on the way to her room when suddenly she stopped and changed her mind. She opened another door and went to sleep in her parents' bed, like when she was still an only child.

She lay down and took in the scent of her father's skin; she turned and smelt her mother's.

"I miss you both so much," she said, bursting into tears again. "Please, I beg you, never abandon me."

Then she wiped her tears on the pillows, clenched her fists and said:

"It's Sergio I have to think of now. Only him!"

4

S HE WOKE AFTER A SLEEP so deep and soothing that she felt as if she had slept for a week. She got up, dressed and ate some stale bread. She put the last remaining pieces of speck and *puccia* into the big jute sack and loaded it on her back.

She closed all the shutters in the house, went out, closed the front door with the big iron key, collected Samson and mounted him.

She made the sign of the cross in the direction of her parents' grave and set off. She turned to look back only once, when, having reached the far end of the meadows, she was ready to begin the descent into the valley.

5

I T WAS MID-MORNING when she reached Bassano del Grappa. The town was in an uproar, stoked by the open-air markets but above all by the masses of migrants trudging haphazardly towards the railway station. They were confused and disorientated and nobody was showing them where to go.

Jole crossed the main square and headed south along the Brenta, which had swollen a great deal thanks to the rain and snow of the last few days.

With her big hat on her head and the now inseparable pendant round her neck, she came to the doors of the convent and pounded on it, her pulse racing.

An eye peered through the little grate in the porter's lodge and simultaneously a voice said:

"*Deus benedicat tibi.* What brings you here?"

Jole made the sign of the cross. "I'm Jole De Boer, sister of the novice Antonia and Sergio, a boy you've been treating in the convent's infirmary."

The nun's eye became less inquisitive and more relaxed. "Please enter."

The door opened and Jole stepped forward, keeping Samson by her side.

An elderly nun appeared from behind one half of the heavy double doors, looked joyfully at Jole and exclaimed:

"Your brother is very well!"

Jole heaved a deep sigh. "I knew it!" she said. She raised her eyes to heaven and a huge smile spread across her face. "I knew it!"

"Leave your horse here and follow me," the nun said.

They crossed a courtyard that contained vegetable patches and vines, passed the guest quarters and went through a creaky little door into a beautiful cloister.

"Look," the nun said, pointing to Sergio, who was sitting on a bench at the far end beside a large magnolia.

Jole ran to her brother. She embraced him, lifted him up, kissed his hair, his forehead, his cheeks. Then she looked at him, deeply moved.

"How are you, little brother?"

Sergio smiled at her, but said nothing. He was well combed and scented and dressed in new clothes, but Jole sensed something different in his facial expression, something that was not right. His right eye was half-closed and there was a strange light in his gaze, as if his thoughts were a long way away.

"Darling, how are you?" Jole asked.

"Unfortunately, he doesn't speak," the elderly nun, who had joined them, said regretfully.

Just then, Jole heard a voice calling her from a distance. She turned.

"Antonia!" she cried, seeing her sister hurrying towards her. "My sister!"

"May God bless you," Antonia said, folding her elder sister in a warm embrace. "You came back."

"All is well, Antonia… All is well."

6

SERGIO SMILED AND AGAIN embraced Jole. For a long time, he clung to her waist, and that encouraged both sisters. And yet Jole had immediately noticed that there was something strange about him: he was slower in his movements, calm where once he had been lively. Antonia asked the elderly nun to keep an eye on her little brother for a few minutes, took her older sister by the hand and led her into the parlour next to the infirmary.

They sat down at a small round table, facing each other. From a fresco above their heads, St Dominic and St Catherine of Siena loomed over them compassionately.

Jole came straight to the point. "What's the matter with Sergio?"

"He's better, as you see, but he doesn't speak," Antonia replied calmly.

"What do you mean, he doesn't speak? Why not?"

"Don't worry. The sister apothecary who treated him says it'll soon pass. It's only a matter of time. His movements, too… he'll be just as lively as before."

Jole was quite agitated now. "But what happened to him? Do they know?"

"No, they don't."

Jole's face darkened. *This is more than a curse!* she thought angrily.

"Thank God Sergio has survived," Antonia went on. "He was in grave danger and his body will bear the marks for a while, but he's survived and he's fine now, and that's all that matters."

"Of course…" Jole sighed, lowering her eyes.

7

A NTONIA TOOK GENTLE HOLD of her sister's hands. "I don't even know where you've been and what you've done, Jole. And so help me God, I don't want to know!"

Jole continued to stare down at the floor.

Antonia looked up at the rosary in St Catherine's hand and said slowly, "I still can't come to terms with the fact that they're dead, Jole... If you only knew how much I've cried. On top of that, Sergio was sick and I didn't know where you were. You might have ended up in some terrible situation."

"Forgive me," Jole said softly, "but there are times when life calls and you can't avoid it. You know something about that, don't you?"

This time it was Antonia who lowered her gaze.

"Thank you for Sergio," Jole said.

They came together again and embraced, warming one another as they had done when they were children and looked to one another for support or compassion, perhaps after one of the two had been reprimanded by Augusto.

"Have you told him about Mamma and Papà?" Jole asked.

"No. He's in no condition to receive news like that. You'll tell him. It's your job."

Jole sighed and felt on her the weight of responsibility that came with being the elder sister. She was well aware that she would have to communicate it all to her little brother, it was an unwritten family duty. This burden was part of her inheritance, too.

"Yes, I'll tell him," she promised.

Antonia squeezed her hands even more tightly than before and smiled at her.

Jole noticed that there were lines at the sides of her sister's eyes. It struck her that time passed even within these walls, however much the talk might be of eternity.

"But how do you really think he is?" she asked. "Do you seriously think he'll get better? He seems so strange to me. It scares me."

Antonia raised her arms to heaven. "I don't know what's in his head. I think he realizes that something strange has happened, he feels it. But he doesn't speak, so he doesn't ask questions. He's confused. According to the apothecary, he might even have partly lost his memory. But I'm convinced he's waiting. He's waiting for someone to tell him something. And take him home soon. But that's up to you, Sister."

Jole slipped her hands from Antonia's and looked down at her palms.

"What is it?" Antonia asked.

Jole bit her lower lip slightly. "I'm not going back to Nevada."

Antonia looked at her without surprise. "And what will you do? Where will you go?"

Jole sighed and was silent for a few moments, knowing that the words she was about to utter were as heavy as a mountain. But she summoned her strength, because she was sure of what she wanted to do. She knew that hers was a considered and unavoidable decision.

She sighed again.

"I'm alone and hungry and I have blood on my hands. Becoming a nun isn't for me, so the only thing I can do is leave. I'm going to America, like they all are. I managed to recover everything that was stolen from Papà. Obviously, Sergio will come with me."

Antonia's eyes watered and her face contracted. She embraced her sister again. "I knew it," she moaned. "I knew it right from the start…"

A heavy silence fell over them, and in that silence was the whole story of the De Boer family, laden with memories but now irreparably shattered. There was also History with a capital H, the History that whirled dizzily around them, shaping the destinies of men and women against their will.

"When will you leave?" Antonia asked.

"Tomorrow. Can I stay here tonight? I really am very tired, Tonia."

8

JOLE WAS GIVEN A TINY CELL and a miserable camp bed. But since she had got used to sleeping in the open air, always on the alert, she found it very comfortable.

Although it was only afternoon, she was so exhausted that she threw herself straight on the bed, hoping to sleep as much as she could and replenish her energy in preparation for her departure. Every time she closed her eyes, though, she saw again those two men bleeding to death and a terrible sensation overwhelmed her. Her heart began to pound and she could not breathe. She was forced to get up again.

Considering her temperament, her honour, her sense of justice towards her mother and father, she felt she had done no more nor less than what had needed to be done. She was convinced she had honoured their memory. Those two thugs had got what they deserved.

In spite of everything, though, she felt drained, as if she were a beech tree perforated by a woodpecker or a pine cone torn apart by a *schirata*, and she wondered why.

Knowing that her parents' killers were dead did not give her the solace she had hoped for when she was following them, hunting them down, vowing to make them suffer a lot. The adrenaline of the pursuit had given way to a tangle of feelings that disturbed her during those hours. With the setting sun, her feelings grew even more acute and from time to time Jole felt actual panic, which she managed to overcome only by opening the window and taking deep breaths of the cold air coming down from the mountains.

What have I gained by it? Have I eliminated the injustices of this disgusting world? Are Mamma and Papà happy now?

Then she calmed down and stood at the window with her jacket and boots on, and continued gazing out at the soft outline of those mountains, so close to heaven and yet at times so hellish.

She wondered if what she was feeling was a sense of guilt, and this question haunted her thoughts for hours, as cruel, pitiless images of Ruggero and Strim in their last moments of life passed endlessly through her head.

I've killed again. Just like two years ago. I've killed again, almost without realizing it. Is it really so easy to become a bad person, God? I don't understand anything anymore. I feel lost in the middle of a snowstorm, as confused as a deer on the plains...

Several times she took hold of her head and shook it roughly, as if to rid it of something that troubled her and prevented her from finding the peace of mind she needed. Then she closed the window, sat down again on the bed and told herself she would fall asleep.

It's only tiredness, just tiredness, she kept saying to herself, taking off her jacket and boots. *It isn't a sense of guilt! I don't feel any sense of guilt. If I've made a mistake, I hope you'll forgive me.*

Falling asleep was not easy, but when at last she drifted off just before eleven, her body fell into a deep oblivion, which not even the tolling of the midnight bells could disturb.

9

T HE NEXT DAY Sergio and Jole both woke feeling rested and had breakfast alone in the refectory. The nuns, who had been awake for hours, had already gathered in the church.

After the morning prayers and the perpetual adoration, Antonia asked permission to stay with her brother and sister for a few more minutes, for the last time. The mother superior gave her consent, so the three De Boers strolled together amid the convent's vines, then sat down side by side in the large cloister.

"I know you aren't allowed personal belongings," Jole said to her sister, "but I want to leave Samson here, in your convent."

Antonia was aware how hard this must be for Jole. She knew she was as fond of her horse as if he were a family member. Jole had rescued Samson when she was a young girl, brought him home, injured, and looked after him. With that horse, she had made journeys, embarked on reckless endeavours, crossed borders, overcome extraordinary obstacles, got to know the world, discovered hate and love, seen death and rediscovered life. With Samson, and even thanks to Samson, she had become a woman.

"I can imagine how much it must hurt to part from him," Antonia said.

Jole closed her eyes and pursed her lips in an attempt to hold back her pain. "You have no idea how much," she said in a low voice. "But I'm sure he'll be fine in your stables."

While they spoke, Sergio looked out at the world, dazed, every now and again trying to catch a midge whirling around him.

One hour later Antonia had to go back to her communal tasks. It was time for Jole and Sergio to leave. They walked to the main door. Antonia accompanied her sister when she went to bid farewell to her faithful Haflinger before he was taken away by the nun in charge of the stables.

Jole put her arms round the neck of her inseparable companion, embraced him and kissed him.

"Forgive me!" she said, sobbing. "Forgive me, but I have to do this. I can't stay here any longer. They'll take care of you, you'll see. I'll miss you so much, my friend. And maybe one day we'll meet again."

Then she walked away from him, not daring to look back, trying in vain to stop crying. She could hear Samson neighing behind her.

"Take care of our brother, Jole, and always trust to the Virgin," Antonia said as they walked to the front door of the convent.

"I will!" she replied, taking Sergio by the hand.

Antonia heaved a deep sigh and lifted her eyes to heaven. "Do you know what to do, whom to turn to for help? And once you get to America, where will you go?"

"Lots of people emigrate every day, and almost none of them know. I'll work it out. I'm not changing my mind. I can't stay here any longer."

Antonia embraced her little brother and said, smiling, "Jole will take care of you. In a few days you'll be even better, you'll see!"

She ran her hand through his fair hair, ruffling it. Jole also smiled.

The two sisters hugged each other tight, as if they did not want to let go. Although they both hoped they might be reunited one day, they were aware that this might be their last embrace.

Sergio, too, clung to them, even though he did not give the impression that he understood what was happening, and the two sisters kissed him tenderly.

"You'll hear from me as soon as I'm settled, Antonia. Someone will help me get in touch with you and will write to you for me, I promise."

"Woe betide you if you don't!" Antonia said, jabbing her chest with a finger. "You hear such incredible things about the New World…"

"I'll miss you. Remember us in your prayers. Remember your family."

"This is my family now, but every day I will pray for the two of you and for Mamma and Papà. May God bless you!"

The nun who had welcomed Jole on her arrival came running up to them, out of breath, carrying a small bag.

"It's from the mother superior," she said. "Something to eat."

Jole thanked her and took the bag, and she and Sergio left the convent. A nun Jole had never seen before waved goodbye and closed the door behind them.

They found themselves out in the street, both carrying bags over their shoulders, ignorant of what awaited them.

She with her broad-brimmed straw hat, he with a felt cap the nuns had got for him.

Jole took tight hold of her brother's hand, leant down towards him and smiled. "Let's go!" she said resolutely.

He nodded and together they walked towards the main square, while she recalled moments spent in the woods with her sister, when their mother would send them to gather blueberries, raspberries, strawberries and elderflowers. "Don't take too long!" she would say, but they would not listen and, once they had gathered the fruit, they would stay there for a long time, playing amid the conifers and the mossy bushes. They would tell each other scary stories, squeeze puffballs to see their spores explode and try to imitate the calls of the animals or the voices of the adults, which would send them into fits of laughter. Once, they found a nutcracker chick fallen from the nest and had taken turns petting it before letting it go. Another time, they had actually kissed each other on the mouth, because they had been curious to know what it would be like. And another time still, they had vowed that they would never part.

"We'll be together for ever!" Jole had said, uttering the words in a solemn tone.

"For ever and ever, for all of our life!" her younger sister had responded.

This was what Jole was thinking about as she walked through the crowds.

*

At that moment, a prayer rose silently in the church, lost among the prayers of all the other nuns, but warmed by the heart of a young woman worried about the fate of her family:

> *O Lord our God,*
> *King of the world, you who made the sun and who light the day,*
> *You who give light to the earth and its peoples,*
> *I beg you to take pity on them.*

10

I T WAS AFTER MIDDAY by the time they reached the railway station.

There were people everywhere, most of them desperate migrants, all huddled together willy-nilly even though there were carabinieri about trying to bring some order to the chaos and confusion.

Around the station, men, women and children were sitting and lying everywhere, on pavements, in squares, on flowerbeds. Many were asleep, others lay worn out by the long journeys they had made or the hunger they had been forced to suffer for hours and even days before getting here. Others were eating, camped out like shepherds, others still running here and there trying to sell off the last things they had left, however useless, to scrape a few lire, or else bargaining with a number of well-dressed people whom Jole immediately recognized as having a degree of authority.

She came to a halt in the station forecourt and sadly surveyed the whole chaotic scene.

"Stay with me!" she advised Sergio, pulling him even closer to her.

She moved forward a few paces and her nostrils were assailed by the smell of the railway, the smoke from the engines, the sweat of all these people.

She plunged into the crowd. She heard the loud whistle of a train. She approached a tired-looking woman who was holding two children by the hand.

"I have to go to America. Who should I speak to?" she asked her, almost screaming to make herself heard over the noise.

The woman did not open her mouth but lifted an arm and pointed to one of the well-dressed men Jole had noticed previously.

These were the emigration agents, unscrupulous men whose business was to arrange the departures and journeys of the poor migrants, selling them tickets that would get them on the train to Genoa and there let them board the liner that would take them to America.

Jole thanked her and approached one of these men. She joined the queue, even though nobody seemed inclined to stay in line. Every now and again, someone would protest and the ensuing argument would turn into a fight. At this point the carabinieri would arrive and attempt to subdue the crowd with their truncheons, hitting out more or less at random, not caring where the blows landed.

When Jole finally managed to get close to one of the emigration agents, she asked:

"How do I get to leave? There's just me and my brother. We want to go to America."

"I've never seen a girl as young as you go to America alone. Where are your parents?"

"They're not here anymore."

"Hmm…" He looked at her suspiciously.

Sergio seemed even more disorientated than she was, which was why Jole wanted to get out of this situation as quickly as possible.

The man gave her a superior, arrogant look. "Do you have money?"

"No, but I have silver and copper."

Now his look turned sly: it was clear she had caught his attention.

He was tall and thin, his nostrils bursting with black hairs, and he spoke with a strong Vicenza accent. He pushed away other people who were clamouring to speak to him, took Jole by the arm and drew her aside.

"Do you have papers?"

"No."

Jole had never thought of this aspect of the matter.

The man winked at her. "If you give me your names and dates of birth, I can get them for you in two hours."

"How much do they cost?" she asked curtly.

The man put his hands over his ears for a moment to shield them from the noise and the yelling. "How much silver do you have with you?"

Jole slipped the knapsack off her back, put her hand inside, felt the four ingots of silver, which were separate from the copper ones, and took one out. "I have this!" she said.

The man took it from her. From the sardonic leer that appeared on his lips and the awestruck expression on his face, Jole knew that she had made him a good offer. But he gave it back to her. "One isn't enough, we're talking about a very long and expensive journey. Come on, I know you have another one, tell me the truth."

Jole looked at him impassively, curious to see who would prevail in these few seconds of silence.

"One isn't enough," he repeated.

Jole plunged her hand back into her knapsack and took out another. "This is the last one!" she said forcefully. "Either this is enough for you, or my brother and I will ask someone else!"

"All right. You can pay the fare to the New World with this, but as far as the papers go, you'll need more. Show me the copper!"

Making sure she was not seen by any of the people crowding around, Jole took out a small ingot.

The man seized it, weighed it in his hand, and gave that one back to her, too. "It'll do. And I don't even want to know how you came by this treasure. I need both your names, along with dates and place of birth."

"Will the papers be real ones? We won't be stopped from going?"

"Totally genuine papers, my girl, stamped by the commune, the prefecture and the Foreign Ministry. You may not have realized this, or maybe you just don't know, but it's in everyone's interest for a lot of people to leave the country. The politicians in Rome are doing everything they can to make sure you go."

Jole looked at him somewhat hesitantly and suspiciously. So suspicious was she that for a moment she considered providing him with false particulars. It was better not to trust anyone, especially after what she had done in the last few days. And she never believed people who talked about things she did not know. But it was too risky.

"Well?" the man said, taking a notebook and a pen from his pocket, ready to write everything down. "I don't have any time to waste!"

"Jole De Boer and Sergio De Boer," she said proudly. "Both born in Nevada. Me on 29 June 1878, him on 8 October 1886."

"So he's twelve?" he asked curiously.

"Yes."

"And doesn't he ever say anything?"

"My brother speaks when I tell him to!"

Jole's tone had turned harsh. She glared at him.

He looked away from her and continued writing their particulars in his notebook.

"And where on earth is this place called Nevada? You know how it is, people come from all over: Belluno, Feltre, Agordo, all the valleys."

"Between the Brenta Valley and the Asiago Plateau."

"Vicenza, then. All right. There's a train at four-thirty. We'll meet half an hour earlier and you'll have your papers and your tickets. They'll explain everything to you on the train. Now give me the two ingots. We'll meet on platform two at four o'clock."

Jole looked him straight in the eyes. "Why should I trust you?"

He opened his arms wide and said calmly, "It's the only thing you can do, my girl."

Jole slowly took out the three ingots and handed them over to him. They shook hands to seal their agreement and he walked off.

After a few metres he turned back to her and repeated, "Four o'clock, platform two!"

Jole nodded, then turned to the crowd. Walking towards the station, she saw a well-dressed gentleman and asked him what time it was.

"Two o'clock," he said, looking at his pocket watch. And he sped away, heading for the centre of the city.

11

HOLDING HER BROTHER'S HAND tightly, Jole entered the station, where the noise was even more deafening because of the constant clanking and grinding and whistling produced by the trains.

She spotted a quieter area, where dozens of people were sitting or lying on the ground, huddled together.

Stay strong, Jole, she told herself. *It'll soon be different. After this journey everything will be better.*

She found a little space among those people and sat down holding Sergio in her arms.

Next to them a young woman, perhaps only a few years older than Jole, was carrying a boy on her back. The boy was amusing himself by blowing into a *cuco*, the little terracotta whistle common in the Veneto.

"He's trying to sound like a locomotive," the woman said to Jole with a smile.

Sergio looked at the boy and above all at his whistle, spellbound.

"Do you like it? Do you want one?" the woman asked him.

"I'm sorry, but we don't have any money," Jole said gently.

"Who said anything about money! I'll give him one. My father made them."

From her pocket she took one shaped like a crow and held it out to Sergio. His face lit up.

Jole thanked the woman and embraced her brother, still hoping that God would bring him back to the way he was before.

She felt fragile, more fragile than ever, what with her see-sawing emotions, filled at times with euphoria and hope and at others falling into gloom and despondency. Suddenly, she felt like crying again. She wondered what was happening to her life, to her family. She wondered if she was dreaming or if it was all true. The tears began to pour out.

The woman put a consoling hand on Jole's shoulder. "Be brave, dear. We'll be better soon, you'll see! Are you going to America, too?"

Jole wiped her eyes and, overcoming her tears, said in a low voice, "Yes. Four o'clock, platform two."

"That's the same train as ours. And you're in the right place: this is the platform. I'm here with my family." One at a time, she pointed to eight people behind her. "Are the two of you alone?"

"Yes. He's my brother," she said softly, recovering a little.

"You can stay with us. There's strength in numbers. We're from Taibon Agordino. What about you?"

"We're from Nevada."

"Where's that?"

Jole laughed. "Nobody's ever heard of it."

They were silent for a few minutes, listening only to the weak sound of the two whistles attempting to drown out the surrounding din.

Jole thanked the woman, who responded with a smile and went on to say, in a self-pitying tone, "Look at what we're reduced to. And how many of us there are… If this is the Italy that Savoy gave us, then I preferred Austria… But we'll be better over there, you bet we will!"

An old man near her, who had listened to her speech, waved his walking stick and cried:

"May God curse the king and all his governments!"

A man huddled next to him, probably his son, reprimanded him. "Careful, the carabinieri will hear you!"

A few minutes later, overwhelmed by the stench rising from that vast mass of human beings and the constant clatter of the steam engines coming and going, Jole, still clinging lovingly to Sergio, unwittingly placed her head on the woman's shoulder and fell asleep. She began dreaming feverishly of images, conversations and emotions that took her back to Nevada, to the past. She dreamt of her mother's face, so like her own, she dreamt about answering her father back after he had reprimanded her and then feeling a great sense of guilt, she dreamt of a huge chestnut tree being uprooted in a blizzard and crashing down onto a flock of sheep, and she dreamt of Samson. She saw him running free and happy in the pastures on the Marcesina plain.

12

I T WAS THE EMIGRATION AGENT who spotted her among all those people.

"Signorina!"

Sergio took the *cuco* from his mouth, shook her to wake her and pointed to the tall man with the hairy nostrils.

"Signorina, your papers and tickets for the journey!" the man said, almost yelling to make himself heard, while around them dozens of migrants sang folk songs from the mountains.

"Your papers and the tickets!" he repeated, close to Jole's ear.

Jole abruptly came to, rubbed her eyes and got to her feet.

He looked at her and smiled. "I'm sorry you're leaving. A pretty girl like you, you'd be sure to find a job here."

Jole ignored this remark. "Give me the papers and tell me what I have to do," she said curtly.

"Here they are. I had to bring your date of birth forward by a year because you need to be twenty-one to leave the country. And I also had to declare that the boy is your parental responsibility."

"What does all that mean?"

"It means you have to say you're twenty-one, not twenty, and that you're the only person in your family taking care of your brother. Have you got that?"

"Yes, all right."

"Anyway, here they are. The papers and the tickets. Can you read?"

"A little."

"A little is better than nothing. I'm sure you're the most educated among this lot." And he pointed to the rest of the people ready to leave. Then he held out a bundle of papers and showed them to her one by one. "Train from Bassano to Padua and from Padua to Genoa with two changes. When you get to the harbour you must ask the shipping company's agents for Sao Paolo, Buenos Aires, Tampico or New York, and show this boarding pass, all right? Anyway, you can't go wrong: just follow this bunch of people and you'll get to America. It's like a river in flood going all the way there from the Veneto, without ever drying up."

Jole listened and looked at him with dull eyes. Once she got to Brazil or wherever, she thought, she would make a new life for herself. She would start all over again from scratch, without ever again making mistakes, certain that God would give her back everything that life and misfortune had taken from her up there, in that place where she would have preferred to live for ever.

"All right!" she said to the agent.

"It's ten past four and the train will be here in a few minutes. Have a good journey and… Lucky you for going to America, or as they all say: 'Merica!"

They shook hands and he gave Sergio's hair a friendly ruffle. The boy glowered back at him.

"One last word of advice, my girl," the man said. "Watch out that you don't catch typhus, and if you hear someone coughing constantly, keep your distance: it's tuberculosis."

13

THE AIR ON THE PLATFORM was cold and damp, imbued with the mood of all those people.

The sky was obscured by the clouds of steam rising from the locomotives and the pervasive smells of iron and coal were strong and persistent.

Jole looked towards the end of the platform and after a while at last saw the engine of their train appear and gradually approach.

It puffed and whistled and, as soon as they saw it, all the other migrants rose excitedly to their feet, singing in unison:

> 'Merica 'Merica
> Where life is grand
> We're off to Brazil
> With family and all.

> 'Merica 'Merica
> Singing as we go
> We're off to Brazil
> To live free and walk tall.

Jole took Sergio's hands. They felt cold and sweaty. She bent down to look into his eyes and wondered what he felt and if he understood any of this. He would get better, she thought, he would start talking again and climbing trees like before, like the little squirrel he was. Brazil would be full of trees you could climb to gather those sweet, fleshy yellow fruits everyone in the station was talking about.

The train arrived, braking with an unbearable metallic screech. It let out a puff of steam so big that for a minute the platform was wrapped in fog.

Jole and Sergio were excited. They had never seen a train at such close quarters. For a moment, the thought of getting in that machine and travelling in it scared Jole.

In the meantime, men and women were shouting and pushing and crowding about the doors of the carriages, which were still closed.

Two mounted carabinieri appeared in an attempt to restore a little order, starting as always to hit the people as if they were animals, before two railway officials and the stationmaster told everyone to move back and prepare to get on calmly, with their tickets in their hands.

Jole gripped the tickets between her teeth, took Sergio in her arms and got in a more or less orderly line with the others.

"Women and children first!" cried the stationmaster, a fat, thickset man with dark cheeks.

The men grumbled, but in the end they did as they had been ordered.

Many were complaining, saying that they had paid a lot of money and deserved a better train than this.

Indeed, apart from the engine – and even that was quite rusty and battered – the train was composed of a few ordinary carriages and a great many animal trucks, or worse still, cattle trucks.

The carabinieri smothered the protests with threats, whirling their truncheons in the air. Once calm had been restored, everyone started getting on the train, although once again with a lot of pushing and shoving.

A railway employee inspected Jole's tickets and told her to get in a different carriage, further towards the back of the train. She hurried to reach the carriage indicated. Before climbing aboard, she made the sign of the cross, and Sergio did the same. Then Jole touched the dandelion pendant around her neck and wondered one last time if she had put everything in her knapsack, including the ingots, the food the nuns had given her and the three larch cones she had gathered the previous evening in Nevada.

With her heart pounding, she removed her hat, put one foot on the bottom step and climbed on.

14

As soon as she had climbed aboard, she pulled up Sergio, who was being squeezed from behind by a braying mob desperate to get on. Both sat down on a wooden bench, as close as possible to the window. Behind them dozens of people poured in, wriggling like trout caught in a fishing net. In a few seconds the space around them was filled with human bodies and unrestrained voices, until not a centimetre was empty. Jole felt suffocated. She moved Sergio closer to the window and tried to open it, but in vain. A man forced the handle and brought it all the way down, and at last a little air entered the carriage, somewhat reviving the stale air around all those poor people. Nothing could be seen outside except the dense, heavy smoke rising a few metres from the engine chimneys then descending quickly to the ground.

Jole recalled the clouds in the sky, when, at high altitude, on days of bad weather, they thicken and descend on the meadows and the valleys, then rise again once the rain has stopped.

She really was about to leave her country, she thought, her land, her people, her past. She was abandoning everything that had formed her and helped her to become a woman. She would be leaving behind her wonderful and unrepeatable moments, unique emotions and feelings, but also terrible adventures, fears and experiences.

She had made a choice, and she had made it with conviction, after hours and days of reflection. She had felt the need to begin a new chapter. In fact, to start a whole new book. To close her eyes on a particular day and open them again on another. She would carry her family in her heart, the smells and memories of her house and her land. She would relive them elsewhere, since she was no longer able to stay here. She would not have been in a position to survive.

She would find and make for herself another homeland, as so many did. Because what everyone had always thought of as their homeland, whether in Nevada or elsewhere in the mountains of the Veneto, no longer existed. Someone had taken everything away from these people, even the right to live where they were born.

The train continued to fill up. Soon there would be no more room in their carriage for anything, not even a chaffinch.

Jole looked Sergio in the eyes and then lifted her hands to her face. She sniffed them and realized, with sadness and joy, that they still had on them the smells of Samson and of St Peter. She hoped that the former, at least, would never fade, and in that way she would always have her horse with her.

She looked out through the window, which faced north. All she saw was steam.

In her carriage it was increasingly hot and the passengers' sweat pervaded every corner of the confined space. She felt as if she had no breath left, no strength.

Everything will be fine, she told herself, closing her eyes. *Everything will be fine.*

15

THE TRAIN WHISTLE blew loudly. Once. Twice. Three times.

They all told each other it was about to leave. Outside, just under the window, the stationmaster with the red hat and brown cheeks blew hard and raised his disk several times.

The wheels squeaked on the rails and the train began to move.

There were some who grew excited, some who started to pray and some who seemed overcome with fear and sadness.

Jole looked again at Sergio and tried, unconvincingly, to smile at him.

The whistle blew again and the train gradually gathered speed, while the clouds of steam began to clear, allowing glimpses of the landscape outside the window.

Some started to sing again, others to drink wine. Jole, crushed further against the glass, looked at the world outside and there, to the north, were the peaks of her mountains. As she gazed at them, she realized that they were getting smaller, moment by moment. The train pulled out of Bassano and headed rapidly south.

Now Jole saw clearly the Grappa massif on the right and the Asiago Plateau on the left.

She realized that she was leaving her mountains and valleys for ever, and she started crying and could not stop.

Just then, a sudden wind rose, a wind so strong that the trees bent beneath it.

There it is, my wind! The soul of the border will guide us.

Sergio, more lost than ever, lightly touched her face with one hand and looked at her freckles, as if spellbound.

"What now?" he asked.

She opened her eyes wide, incredulous. He had spoken!

"Jole, what now?" he repeated.

Jole leant over him, hugged him tight and said:

"Now for the future!"

Acknowledgements

A special thank you to my friend Mauro Corona, a man of rare loyalty.

And thank you, too, to Matteo Bisato, Marco Busatta, Angelo Chemin, Giuseppe Mendicino, Angelo Troi, Daniele Zovi.

PUSHKIN PRESS

Pushkin Press was founded in 1997, and publishes novels, essays, memoirs, children's books—everything from timeless classics to the urgent and contemporary.

Our books represent exciting, high-quality writing from around the world: we publish some of the twentieth century's most widely acclaimed, brilliant authors such as Stefan Zweig, Marcel Aymé, Teffi, Antal Szerb, Gaito Gazdanov and Yasushi Inoue, as well as compelling and award-winning contemporary writers, including Andrés Neuman, Edith Pearlman, Eka Kurniawan, Ayelet Gundar-Goshen and Chigozie Obioma.

Pushkin Press publishes the world's best stories, to be read and read again. To discover more, visit www.pushkinpress.com.

THE SPECTRE OF ALEXANDER WOLF
GAITO GAZDANOV
'A mesmerising work of literature' Antony Beevor

SUMMER BEFORE THE DARK
VOLKER WEIDERMANN
'For such a slim book to convey with such poignancy the extinction of a generation of "Great Europeans" is a triumph' *Sunday Telegraph*

MESSAGES FROM A LOST WORLD
STEFAN ZWEIG
'At a time of monetary crisis and political disorder... Zweig's celebration of the brotherhood of peoples reminds us that there is another way' *The Nation*

THE EVENINGS
GERARD REVE
'Not only a masterpiece but a cornerstone manqué of modern European literature' Tim Parks, *Guardian*

BINOCULAR VISION
EDITH PEARLMAN

'A genius of the short story' Mark Lawson, *Guardian*

IN THE BEGINNING WAS THE SEA
TOMÁS GONZÁLEZ

'Smoothly intriguing narrative, with its touches of sinister,
Patricia Highsmith-like menace' *Irish Times*

BEWARE OF PITY
STEFAN ZWEIG

'Zweig's fictional masterpiece' *Guardian*

THE ENCOUNTER
PETRU POPESCU

'A book that suggests new ways of looking at the world
and our place within it' *Sunday Telegraph*

WAKE UP, SIR!
JONATHAN AMES

'The novel is extremely funny but it is also sad and
poignant, and almost incredibly clever' *Guardian*

THE WORLD OF YESTERDAY
STEFAN ZWEIG

'*The World of Yesterday* is one of the greatest memoirs of the twentieth
century, as perfect in its evocation of the world Zweig loved, as it is
in its portrayal of how that world was destroyed' David Hare

WAKING LIONS
AYELET GUNDAR-GOSHEN

'A literary thriller that is used as a vehicle to explore big
moral issues. I loved everything about it' *Daily Mail*

FOR A LITTLE WHILE
RICK BASS

'Bass is, hands down, a master of the short form, creating in a few pages
a natural world of mythic proportions' *New York Times Book Review*